Death Cracks The Case

A Taylor Texas Mystery

VIKKI WALTON

Morewellson, Ltd.

Death Cracks The Case

For permission requests, write to the publisher:

Attention: Permissions Coordinator
Morewellson, Ltd.
P.O. Box 49726
Colorado Springs, Colorado 80949-9726

ISBNs:
978-1-950452-51-4 (electronic publication edition)
978-1-950452-52-1 (standard trade publication edition)

Cover design by The Cover Vault
Formatting by Wild Seas Formatting; Rik Hall

CHAPTER ONE

Christie grabbed her favorite pair of jeans from the closet. She stepped into each leg before yanking them up over her hips and preparing to zip them up. The zipper stuck about halfway up.

What the--?

Christie unzipped the tight blue jeans, adjusted them, and tried again. The zipper still wouldn't close at the top. Going over to the bed, she laid down and could zip the pants up.

Stupid dryer.

But in her heart, Christie knew it wasn't the dryer. Ever since she'd begun to date Bryson, her clothes had become snugger. While she'd always been a tall, big-boned girl, her previous work with hospice patients had kept her fit, so she hadn't had to worry too much about gaining weight. Lifting and lowering patients daily had given her a lot of muscle in place of fat.

Now that she'd returned home to Comfort,

she hadn't the daily strain, though she still had the care and feeding of her own horse and working with the horses at the nonprofit. But once she'd taken over as executive director, more of her time had been spent sitting in front of a computer or connecting with donors.

Her role as director meant more lunches or dinners out, and she wasn't used to the constant networking and schmoozing. Often before, she'd be so tired at the end of the day that she'd grab a hearty soup and salad or fix a quick sandwich. Breakfast was comprised of a large coffee and a granola bar she'd grab as she headed out the door to work. Couple the decrease in physical activity and the increase in so much food, it was no surprise she'd been gaining some weight recently.

She rose from the bed and went over to the mirror. She pointed at her reflection. "Get a handle on this before it gets out of hand." Just as she stuck out her tongue, she heard boots climbing the wooden stairs to her home. She still loved her elevated cob home, but she realized that it wasn't going to be practical as she grew older.

What had she been thinking?

Bryson had come over and they would be taking the horses out riding Pop's property before heading over toward the equine nonprofit. Her team of volunteers were great, but a lot had taken off to enjoy the long weekend as it was an unofficial signal of kids getting back into school fully and leaving behind the summer schedule. Christie was happy to give them the time off as she would enjoy some physical work this afternoon, mucking out stalls and putting some horses out in the back corral.

When she'd told Bryson that she'd be on duty over the weekend, he said he'd join her as he didn't have any electrical jobs or anything else planned. This would work well, as it meant that Bryson could help in the morning before Tom, the night guy, took over for the evening. It was also good that she wouldn't have to stop working, as Bryson would bring her dinner for that evening, so one less thing to think about.

Christie grabbed a scrunchy and pulled her hair up into a messy bun before heading to the door. Bryson stood with his back to her, most likely gazing out toward the hill country view with its scrub oak and the sun's light peeking through the trees. Christie wanted to get started earlier so it would be cooler in the barns. Even in September, the temperature was still hot and mucking the barns meant lots of sweaty work ahead.

She smiled at the man standing outside. Butterflies in her stomach still made her realize the attraction she felt for him, even though she'd tried denying it for the months they've been seeing each other. Her heart threatened to override her head when it came to love. Even with Lana throwing up her hands as she'd say, "God literally brought this man through your front door, what more confirmation do you need?"

But Christie knew that she had waited a very long time to even consider the idea of spending the rest of her life with someone, and she was in no hurry now. She grabbed a visor as he turned to see her, a grin growing on his face as she moved closer to the glass-paned door.

"Morning, sweetie." He kissed her on the cheek. "I'll spare you the coffee breath."

"Morning to you, too. Come in. I only need to grab my old boots and I'll be ready to go."

"Sounds good. I saddled Champ for you."

Christie smiled. "Thank you. And I don't mind coffee breath." She kissed him on the mouth. They'd been taking a class on love languages, and she'd found out that hers were acts of service while his was quality time. So they'd both been making an effort for the other. She didn't know how hard it was for him, but as someone that had spent much of her life alone, it was definitely an adjustment to include him more in her daily outings and routines. She was used to going and doing, so bringing him along was another change that she was willing to make in her life.

The pair descended the stairs and made their way to the barns where Bryson's horse, Spirit, and Champ stood waiting at the back of Bryson's trailer. She was surprised she hadn't heard him drive up or that Pop's dogs, Mutt, and Jeffrey, hadn't raced over to her house barking their hello's. Pop must have them inside with him.

Christie swung up on Champ's back as Bryson did the same on Spirit, as the horses moved their heads with the grasp of the reins. She made a clicking sound as she moved the reins to the right, away from the back of the trailer.

"Okay to run by Pop's place on the way?"

"Sure."

"Just a reminder, though. No getting off our horses or he'll trap us into breakfast."

Bryson stuck out his bottom lip. "But he makes such a good breakfast."

"Sorry, not today."

As the horses made their way over toward Pop's place, Mutt raised his head, furry tail thumping on the wooden porch while Jeffrey stood up from the porch, tail wagging back and forth.

Christie yelled out, "You two are getting lazy."

Jeffrey barked back a reply before turning in circles and laying down on a sunny spot on the porch. Pop's truck wasn't there, so he must have already left to head into town for coffee with his cronies.

That benefited them, as Christie knew they'd be spending a lot of time chatting if Pop had been at home, but she always wanted to make the time for her father. The fact is that she'd seen too many people who regretted not taking the time to spend with their family member, who was now leaving this life. And it wasn't just those who were elderly. It was younger people that everyone thought would have a long life ahead of them, only to discover that their loved one had a fatal disease or been the victim of someone who'd been driving distracted or impaired. She never wanted to say that she hadn't made time to call or stop by and visit with Pop.

They rode in companionable silence as Christie dictated on her phone on any places where fencing needed repair or if there was a spot that looked out of the ordinary. She'd just made a note on fixing a fence post when Bryson spoke.

"Oh, I wanted to let you know that I'm doing some work over at the Fat Cat Winery and was telling the owners about the equine rescue. Abby said she'd love to hear more about it, and I'm pretty sure a substantial donation would be offered as well."

"That's great news. When we get to Horse Haven, give me the details and I'll set up a time to have them come visit the rescue."

"I think it would be better if you went out there first. They're really busy with the expansion and I think it would be more low-key. Plus, I think it may be better to speak to Abby and let her take the lead on it."

"Well, if they're busy, should I wait until a better time?"

Bryson shook his head. "No, she said she'd love for you to come out and see the place. They took over for the previous owners and she's considering doing an event to introduce it with the new name. When I shared about the successful event you held last year for the rescue, Abby was all ears. She's thinking of having the event be a paid event with part of the proceeds going to the horse rescue."

"Wow, that's amazing. I wonder why, as they don't even know us. But that would be awesome. Then I definitely want to get her on my schedule to visit next week. I could kiss you."

"You could." He winked.

"Later." She chuckled.

"I'm going to hold you to that." He grinned. "Oh, and a heads-up, her husband is a ...how to put this politely, well, you'll see."

"Uh, oh. So, I'll have to deal with a difficult person too? I think I'd rather pass."

Bryson moved Spirit closer to Champ. "Pass on a six-figure donation?"

"Seriously?"

He nodded. "I don't know the full story, but I think one of them came into some money, hence the move here and the purchase of the winery. They don't need to do it, it's more like a pet project. I don't want to share too much about it, but I think her husband is dealing with some PTSD issues and this helps give him the purpose he needs. From what she shared, it was either here or a place in France or Italy and they decided it was going to be enough headache without all the other issues."

"I wouldn't want to live overseas, but it would be nice to do some traveling there." She sighed.

"What's the matter?"

Christie responded, "I just wish they'd hurry up on hiring a new director for the rescue."

"You know they aren't going to hurry on it. They want you to stay on. Plus, what would you do if you weren't involved with it—go back to nursing?"

"I've considered it, but as I get older, I think my nursing days are past. But I need to do something more active, my pants are getting tight and can only blame it on the dryer so many times."

"Well, I think you look lovely, no matter what." His eyes met hers, and she knew he meant it. "However, I've been noticing it a bit too."

"That's rude." She responded.

He laughed and patted his stomach. "No, not you. Me! I love the delicious pies you make, but between them and all the good home-cooking from you or Pop, I may have to change a notch in my belt or consider taking up wrestling."

Christie laughed. "Okay, well, now that we've admitted it, we both need to become better about our eating habits. So, no more pie—"

"Ack!" He pretended that he'd been shot, falling over to land close to Spirit's neck. The horse whinnied at his movement. Bryson sat back up, patting the horse's neck.

Christie rolled her eyes. "Come on. We have to be serious. We can't keep eating lots of fried foods and desserts without gaining weight. If we expect to lose these added pounds, we've got to be more diligent on our diet."

"Ugh, how I hate that word. It has the word die in it because when you're on one, you just want to give up."

"Good grief. Diet is only a word. We're all on a diet. It's just some have a healthy diet, some have an okay diet, and some have a poor diet. Sugar decreases your immune system, so this would be a good time to cut back as the temps get colder and illnesses make the rounds."

"Fine, but you promised me a new pie later this month for my birthday." He made a face with a pouting mouth.

"All right, pie on your birthday, but that's it. And we need to up our vegetables too. Agreed?"

"Okay, sure. I know that we need to take care of ourselves, so we'll have a long time to spend together." He responded.

She smiled. "I agree. Now, see if you can stay up with me, old man." She yelled, "Hah" and prodded Champ into a gallop.

"Hey, no fair!"

CHAPTER TWO

Christie rubbed the tension from her neck and shoulders. The work with the horses over the weekend had been hard physically but also a good reminder of how out of shape she was getting. She'd have to figure out some way to take better care of herself and get more physical activity in her day. Maybe getting a standing desk converter would at least help some with the time spent sitting in front of her computer.

After placing a call to the winery, the person answering the phone placed her on hold with some classical music playing in the background.

A voice came on the line, "Hello, this is Abby."

"Hello, Abby. This is Christie Taylor with the equine rescue, Horse Haven. Bryson recommended I contact you. He said you might need some assistance concerning an event you're thinking of hosting."

"Oh, yes. Hold on and I'll move to some place

where it's quieter."

Christie could hear voices in the background, with an angry, deep male voice yelling. Had Abby forgotten to mute her phone? It was hard not to be shocked as the man's anger spewed into name-calling. Christie wasn't sure what she should do. Thinking fast, she ended the call. Maybe Abby would think she hadn't overheard the conversation.

She'd punched the number back in when her phone rang. "Hello?"

"This is Abby. Sorry, the phone must have dropped the call. It does that sometimes."

"Yes, it does that here as well, depending on certain areas of the barns." Christie replied. She was thankful that Abby either thought she hadn't heard the furious exchange or was simply going to avoid speaking about it.

Abby continued. "Anyway, I'd love for you to come out and take a look around and let me know what you think. Of course, I want to hear more about the rescue as well. I've always wanted horses, but my husband, Dax, doesn't want to take any on because of the amount of work we already have on our plates.”

“Horses are definitely a lot of work. If you get a chance, we have some you could ride if you’d like that.”

“Maybe, not sure when I’d have time, but appreciate the offer.”

“Well, know that it’s available. Just be good to give us a few days’ heads up. Anyway, would be happy to come share about what we’re doing and our fundraising event. When would be a good time?”

“I know it’s last minute, but what about this afternoon?”

“Um, what time?” Christie moved her mouse to bring her computer to life and looked at her calendar. Most weeks she kept Mondays free, but she wanted to check just in case. Sure enough, the day was clear.

“You could come over around two this afternoon. Usually that’s the time we take a break, and the crew often will eat a later lunch around then. Would that work for you?”

"Yes. I can do that." Christie said.

"Do you need the address or directions?"

"Bryson said you're out toward Center Point. I can get directions from him."

"Oh, yes, of course. How do you know Bryson?"

Christie hesitated. Should she say they were dating? Right now, she wanted to keep their relationship between the two of them and close family. Plus, since he was doing electrical work, she didn't want it to cause any issues if they didn't move forward on donating to the rescue. "His company did the electrical work here at the rescue."

"Oh, yes. I recall hearing something about an incident that happened. Should I be concerned?"

"No. That was nothing to do with him or his company. They do excellent work." Christie replied.

"Good. I would hate to have to start over with another firm. Must run. See you at two. Bye!"

"Bye."

The call ended.

"Okay then. This should be interesting." Christie spent the rest of the morning going over the various logs from the weekend, setting up the paperwork for two new pony arrivals, and signing off on an adoption. One of the best things of the rescue was when they could bring horses that had been neglected back to health so that they go to good owners. The adoption fees also helped offset some costs for feeding and any veterinary services.

Christie saved what she was working on and went to the breakroom to fix something to eat. Sticking some Ezekiel bread in the toaster, she pulled out the prepared containers of smashed avocado, pickled red onions, roast chicken strips, and spinach. Grabbing a plate, she took the bread out once the toaster oven pinged, spreading the yummy avocado on the crusty brown bread. She then constructed her avocado toast, layering the spinach and shredded chicken on top of the toast, finishing it by a light sprinkle of Tony's Cajun spices and salt.

Lana entered the room. "Oh, that looks

yummy."

Christie held the plate out to Lana. "You want one? I can make more."

Lana shook her head. "No, thanks. I had a snack earlier. I tell you, school gets harder every year or I'm getting older." She slumped into a nearby chair, rolling her shoulders back before doing some arm stretches.

Christie's eyebrows rose.

"Ha ha. You do not know how I miss sleeping in."

"You may complain, but you know you love it." Christie picked up the toast and took a delicious bite of the savory blend.

Lana moved forward on her chair, stretching her legs out in front, and then rotating her ankles. "I do. I never realized what I was missing until I moved here. It was as if I'd finally come home and now I'm right where I need to be. Plus, it's not like I'd get to sleep in with kids either, but maybe a bit more now that they're older."

"Before you know it, they'll be heading off into the world."

Lana sunk her head into her hands. "Don't remind me. It seems like yesterday that they were still toddlers. I can't even imagine Allie and Trey flying the coop. But I have to really focus on them now. You know you'd think that kids need more parent involvement when they're younger, but the older I get, I see the need to really instill values into them and especially Allie as she moves into her teenage years. Then there's Trey. I have him in lots of good opportunities but--"

Christie knew what Lana had left unspoken. Boys needed a father and with her husband killed during his tour, Lana had put all of her efforts into being there for her children. While Curtis, Lana's grandfather spent time with Trey, he wasn't able to do as much with the boy. Having no kids of her own, Christie didn't know what Lana was dealing with, but she could be a supportive friend to her. She nodded and swallowed before responding.

"I'll say this. Even though I'd lived in Comfort growing up, it felt so good to settle back down here. What's on your schedule today?"

As Christie devoured her avocado toast, Lana

went over the day and summarized the week. Christie wiped her mouth with a napkin. "Sounds good. When the board meets Thursday, we can let them know we're heading into the last quarter doing well in every area."

"All down to your leadership."

Christie held a finger up in front of her mouth. "Shush. I want them to find another director to replace me, remember?"

"Come on, Christie. Why? You know you love it here."

"I do. But I want, I don't know. Something different. Plus, I can still volunteer."

"That something different walked through your door. When are you going to say yes to that poor man and put him out of his misery?"

"Please don't. I have to go at my own pace."

"At your pace, you'll both be dead before you realize what a great guy he is. Don't wait." Lana popped up from the chair. "Back to work. I have one foal that is really struggling after its recent birth."

"Oh, no. Do you think it will be okay?"

"Yes, we're doing some taping on his haunches, so that should help."

Christie moved her plate to the side. "I still don't quite understand how that tape works."

Lana stood. "It's basically bringing the hair follicle up, thus increasing blood flow, which helps with any pain or stress on that area. It'll help him heal a lot quicker. I thought you'd used it before."

"I have but didn't really know that much about it other than it was supposed to help, so thought I'd give it a shot."

"Speaking of shots, you up for some target practice later this week?"

"Maybe. I may get roped into helping put some food up for this winter."

Lana stretched. "I hear ya on that. Curtis has already been talking to me about it, too. Well, let's catch up more later."

"Sounds good. Also, as an F-Y-I, I'm headed out to the Comfort Point winery. I'm getting a tour and possibly a donation."

"Sounds good. Bring me back a bottle of

wine." Lana winked.

"I didn't think you drank?"

"Only on special occasions."

"Such as?"

"Such as when I'm in the mood for a glass of wine with my pasta. Or when it's 'none-o-ya-biz' time."

"Funny. Well, I'm not going to ask, so if she gives me some, I'll pass it along to you, wino." Christie winked.

The drive to the Fat Cat Winery was uneventful. On arrival, Christie was directed to a large barn by one of the crew working on the grounds, adding in some perennial plants. Christie made her way over to where Abby was sweeping the floor of some debris. Her back was turned to Christie and her plaid shirt sleeves rolled up high on her arms. As she moved, Christie glimpsed a series of ugly bruises on Abby's right arm. As she moved the broom, Abby spied Christie.

"Oh, hello. Is it two already? Time got away from me." She set the broom up against the wall and, with a swift movement, lowered her shirt sleeves, but not before Christie spied bruises on her other arm.

The woman caught Christie's eye. "I'm a walking bruise right now. I keep running into everything." She pulled the other sleeve down. "How about we grab some iced tea or soda in the office and then we'll do the tour?"

"Sounds good."

Christie followed Abby into the bowels of the large facility with huge drums on one side that must hold the wine in various stages. Metal steps led up to a couple of older-looking ones with a small, grated landing at the top.

In the office, Christie accepted a bottle of unsweetened iced tea from Abby. She took a swig. Oh, how she wanted to add sugar, but forgoing sugary drinks was a simple way to cut down on calories. They went outside to where a group of men stood next to the end of a row of grapevines.

Abby pointed toward the leafy, green vines. "This will be our first harvest. We're really excited. We've had the soil analyzed and we think the terroir is unique and will—"

"I'm sorry, what?" Christie asked.

"Oh, the terroir. It's a French word. Basically, it is the environmental characteristics that produce the result. So that can include the specific topography, the soil components, weather, etc. I believe the first owner didn't realize the gold mine they had. They didn't give it enough time for the vines to produce a good batch."

Christie shielded her eyes, scanning the rows of vines, heavy with leaves and fruit. "It looks like they're very healthy."

"Yes, the first year we got here, we basically checked everything out and then we burnt a lot of it away."

"What? Why would you do that?"

"To create biochar. It helps to nourish the vines when they need it as well as helping with water retention. As you can imagine, that's important here in Texas. Once we did that, the vines started thriving."

"Interesting. I never knew this. Excuse me, but I thought y'all had recently moved here but that sounds like it happened over years?"

Abby nodded. "You're correct. When we found out about the property, we wanted to ensure it would produce so we worked with the current owner on it. We had things going some of the time but mostly it was allowing the ground to rest and create the right conditions."

"The terroir?"

"Yes, to a point. We simply helped it to become all it could be."

"You certainly know a lot about this."

Abby smiled. "I never do anything half-way. I study it thoroughly to ensure I'm getting it right. I don't want any mistakes."

"I hear you. I'm the same way."

"Now, Christie, I've prattled on long enough about what we're doing. Let's get back in the office where it's cooler. Fall is definitely nicer temperature-wise, but I'm still not used to this Texas humidity."

Back in the office, Christie gave the spiel about the equine rescue and how it was helping the horses but also about the other programs with special needs individuals and veterans experiencing post-traumatic stress.

Abby sat back in her chair, clasping her hands together in front of her. "Wow. I had no idea you all did so much good work there."

Christie couldn't help beaming with pride. They really did do a lot of good for the surrounding community. "In addition, we work with the local 4H, the vet schools, etc. so we really keep our costs down and our volunteers are wonderful."

"I'd love to come over and see it sometime." Abby said.

"You're welcome to stop by. Midmornings or afternoons are usually best if you want to avoid the morning madhouse of getting all the animals fed and their stalls mucked out."

"Great." Abby stood.

The door to the office flew open, hitting the wall with a bang. A man, his face contorted in anger, burst into the room. He yelled, "What did you do?

CHAPTER THREE

After Abby quickly excused herself and left with the man, Christie was left wondering if she should stay or leave. Finally, a young man came in and announced that there had been some issues with one of the vats and that Abby would contact her at a later time when she would provide a donation to the charity.

Christie thanked him and made her way back to her truck. What could have happened that caused such upset? Was that Abby's husband? If so, Christie would hate to be around him all the time.

She drove away from the winery, turning onto the main road. Lost in thought, she came back to attention when she felt the truck shudder as the truck pulled to the right.

Crud. Must be a blow-out.

Christie slowed the truck down and eased the vehicle as far as she could onto the shoulder, where she threw the truck into park. Opening the door, she walked around the front to see the flat tire.

She must have driven over a nail or there'd been a puncture she hadn't seen. Thankful that Pop had instructed her on changing a tire when she was a teenager, Christie retrieved the spare tire. She rolled it to the front before grabbing the jack from the back. She was screwing the last lug nut back on when the sounds of sirens filled the air.

Wiping her hands on a red cloth she kept in her disaster kit, Christie watched as emergency vehicles approached, rushing by her. They slowed, only to turn onto the road that led to the winery.

Oh no, had something happened?

Christie labored to put the punctured tire back into her truck bed, debating on what she should do. She stared as the ambulance turned onto the drive for the Fat Cat Winery. Curiosity got the best of her, and she rushed back to the scene. Parking her truck out of the path of the vehicles, she saw a young man sitting on a bench close to the entrance. He held a once white cloth now stained dark to his head as a technician pointed a penlight in his eyes.

Did this have something to do with Abby's husband bursting into the office, or was this completely separate from the incident?

Spying another man exiting the barn, she sprinted over to him. "Hi, I'm Christie. I was just here and saw the emergency vehicles. Is he okay?"

She pointed toward the man with the bloodied cloth.

He nodded, adjusting his ball cap, before replying. "He was headed up to one of the vats when he tripped and hit his head. But he's tough. He'll be okay."

"Yikes. That sounds dangerous."

"Not really. Though it seems a bit off."

Christie replied, "Why's that?"

"He's a careful guy. Plus, I could see him possibly tripping down the stairs, but up them? I don't know." He shrugged. "That's life. Stranger accidents have happened."

"I know what you mean." She replied.

He made to get in his truck.

"Wait. Do you mean in general or here?"

He slung himself onto the truck's seat. "I guess both. We've been having some strange things happening, but I would chalk that up to Dax pushing so hard."

"Doesn't sound like you like him much."

He shrugged. "it's a job. I don't have to like the boss."

"What about Abby? Isn't she your boss too?"

"I wish." He caught himself before returning an embarrassing gaze to Christie. "I don't know why she puts up with him. Especially with the— Never mind."

Christie lowered her voice. "I saw bruises on her arm today when I arrived."

His jaw clinched, and Christie realized that he was fighting back any response. Was Dax abusive?

"Listen, I need to go. I only have a short time to get these errands done." He reached to close the door, but Christie grabbed the frame. She needed to know what she was getting into if she accepted any donation from them.

"Are you saying Dax is dangerous?"

"You didn't hear it from me." He pulled the door closed.

Christie turned to spy Abby standing near the young man, whose head now bore a bandage on it. The woman looked up and when she saw Christie; she spun back toward the injured man. Had something that Abby had done caused the man to be harmed? She wish she knew what Abby was supposed to have done. One thing Christie knew, though.

It looks like money didn't equate to happiness.

~

Back at the rescue, Christie got roped into helping Lana with a couple of new arrivals. She finally turned out the office lights at seven, just as her phone dinged with a text.

Home yet?

No.

I could pick something up.

Christie had looked forward to soaking in a hot bath, but the idea of seeing Bryson as well as not having to cook was appealing. She texted him back.

Sure. You pick.

Okay. See you soon.

Deciding to check in on Pop, she punched in his number. The phone rang for a bit before he answered.

"Hey, darlin.'"

"Hi Pop. Just thought I'd call and check in with you. Everything good?"

"Thanks, sweetie. Yep, Curtis and I went into Kerrville today and had lunch and now I'm watching football on television."

Christie knew from his words and the sound of his voice, it meant he was snoozing in front of the TV.

"Okay, well, didn't want to take you away from anything. I'm on my way home and thought I'd call while I was thinking about you and wanted to make sure you're okay."

"Fit as a fiddle. Your fella coming over to see

you tonight?"

Christie replied, "Yes, he's bringing over some take out for dinner since I had such a long day."

"Well, good. He's a good catch. You don't want to wait too long, Christie."

"Pop—"

"Just saying. You either need to fish or cut bait. That man is head-over-heels with love, and you don't often get lots of second chances of finding a good man like him."

Christie started to spout off that she would decide if and when she decided to marry, but bit back the retort.

Pop continued, "Ya know, I ain't getting any younger. You need someone in your life. I want to know you'll be taken care of when I'm gone."

Christie smiled to herself. It didn't matter that she had been an independent woman for all these years. To Pop, she'd always be his baby. Whereas she might have been upset with him thinking she needed anyone to take care of her, the older she'd gotten, she'd realized that it wasn't about the big things. He knew she could handle that. It was knowing that she had someone who would always be there, no matter what.

"Listen, I gotta run. Talk later, okay?"

"Hey, before you go, I've been hankering for some pie. Whatcha making this weekend?"

"Nothing."

"What?"

"Cutting back on sweets for a while. And fried foods too."

"What are you saying? Life ain't worth living without some good pie. Or fried taters and gravy."

Christie chuckled. "Don't worry. I've already promised Bryson I'd make pie for his birthday."

"I could tell you something he'd love to get for a present—tell him yes."

"Pop, you're incorrigible."

Pop answered. "Is there any other way to be? Gotta go. Nature calls. Love ya, sweetie."

The call ended.

Christie drove home to find Bryson waiting when she arrived. She stepped down from her truck. "How did you get here so soon?"

"I was already at the Chinese restaurant

ordering. I know Mondays are busy days and I'd stopped by, and they told me you'd gone out to Fat Cat. I know how you hate talking to donors, so I took the initiative to have a meal waiting for you when you got home. I think this counts for acts of service."

Christie groaned. "Please don't tell me we're keeping score. I don't think I can handle the pressure."

He laughed. "No. Just want to make sure I'm on the right track with things you want as you do so much for yourself. Hard to find things to do for you."

"Well, not having to think about dinner is certainly one of my favorite acts of service, so thanks. I appreciate it."

He held up one of the bags, "And I was good. White rice versus fried rice."

Christie smiled. "Thanks." She took the bag he offered her and mounted the steps to her lit-up house. Bryson was right. Having a couple of lights on timers made all the difference of arriving to a welcoming home. Inside, she crossed over to turn on the kitchen lights and set the bag down on the table.

"What do you want to drink?"

"Got iced tea?"

Christie pulled two tall glasses from the cabinet. "Yes, but it's unsweetened."

"Ugh. Will I get my hand slapped if I add a bit of sugar to it?"

She laughed. "No."

After pouring tea in the glasses, they started in on some warm hot and sour soup as the pair talked a bit about their day. Then Bryson brought up the incident at the winery.

Christie said, "Yes, I'd had a flat right after I left, so I saw the emergency vehicles go by."

"You should have called me. I'd have come fix your tire." He set the soup aside, opening the container of rice, along with one filled with beef and broccoli.

Christie wiped her mouth with a napkin before replying. "I didn't need help. Pop taught me how to change a tire when I was young."

Bryson reached over and put his hand on

Christie's. "Listen, I know you're capable. More than capable of any woman I know. That doesn't mean you have to do everything yourself. I want to be helpful. I want you to depend on me."

Christie swallowed before sighing. "I've been on my own for a long time. You know that I'm not only independent but also self-sufficient."

"And I love that about you. I do. It's part of who you are and why I love you. I'm just saying that you don't have to do everything. I'm willing and able to ease some of your burden."

Christie sighed again. "Can we talk about something else? For instance, what happened at the winery? I saw that one guy had been hurt. Do you know anything about it?"

Bryson pulled his hand back, picking up a spoon to dish out the rice. "From what I understand, he tripped or fell and hit his head on the metal railing by one of the vats. There'd been some commotion about someone adding more sugar or something to the vat. I don't know. Not much knowledge of wine and how it's made." Bryson opened a paper envelope, placing an egg roll on Christie's plate while putting another one on his own plate. He dipped his egg roll in sweet and sour sauce and took a bite.

"Oh, that must have been what Abby's husband meant when he came into the office."

He lifted his eyebrows in question while he continued chewing.

Christie continued, "He'd stormed in while we were talking and said, 'what did you do' to Abby. It was pretty shocking, to be honest. He didn't even calm down after he saw me there."

"Hm. I don't know anything about that, but I know that it's a pretty complex process. Make a mistake, and it could cost you hundreds, if not thousands, of dollars."

"I found it interesting. Abby told me they were extremely excited about this batch as they had done some work on the soil and that the terror, no wait, terroir makes a big impact on production."

"Yes, I think they're trying to get some kind of certification or designation. That's not making their neighbor incredibly happy, I can tell you that."

"What do you mean?"

"They're in litigation because of some property boundary issues. Not sure what has been happening on it, but it's gotten pretty ugly from what I've heard from some of their crew. They say that Dax and Abby are at each other's throats because of it. Lots of money involved."

"That could explain the bruising." Christie said to herself.

"Bruising? What do you mean?"

"I think Dax may be abusive. I saw bruises on her arms today and later I realized they looked like the prints of grabbing someone. When Abby saw me looking, she dropped the sleeves of her shirt down to cover them."

Bryson shook his head. "I hear what you're saying but nope. Dax definitely has a temper and flies off the handle, but I can't see him hurting anyone, let alone Abby, physically." He shook his head. "Naw. Not him. I'd stake my reputation on it."

"But what about the bruising on her arm?"

"We don't know how they got there. What did she say?"

"She said that she got bruises all the time because of the work."

He sat back in his chair. "See, there you go. I get bruises or cuts all the time. It's a hazard of the job. And I've seen some doozy of bruises you've gotten while working with the horses."

"I guess you're right. But then why try to cover them up like she did?"

He shrugged. "Who knows why anyone does anything?"

Bryson's question repeated in her mind.

Who knows why anyone does anything?

All she knew was that she was tired and maybe she'd seen something that wasn't there, thus jumping to the wrong conclusions. Tomorrow she'd be thinking clearer. But if there were lots of troubling incidents happening at the winery, did it mean that more were on the way?

CHAPTER FOUR

The following morning Christie was at work editing the monthly donation letter when a knock came on her office door.

"Come in!" She normally kept her door open but she'd closed it so she could concentrate. Because she'd let the staff know it meant she didn't want to be disturbed unless the barn was on fire, the person must have something important to tell her.

Her new assistant, Rene, peeked her blonde head in the door. Her freckled face bore an apologetic expression. "Sorry to interrupt, but Abby's here to see you. I told her to wait downstairs so I could see if you were available."

"Thanks, Rene. I'll come down in just a minute."

"Great." The tanned young woman closed the door behind her.

Christie surveyed her desk, covered with paperwork, and the debris of coffee cups and a cardboard slab of a rice cake with two bites missing. Christie picked up the rice cake, contemplating taking another bite, when she shook her head and said, "Nope." She pitched the item into the silver trash container next to her desk, determining to never buy the item again. She'd chew on cardboard first if she got desperate. Whoever made those must lack any joy in life. Christie dusted her hands off and stood.

Better to have the meeting with Abby in the conference room. She closed the green folder open on her desk and locked the office door behind her before making her way downstairs. Abby stood chatting with Rene and the pair were quite animated in whatever they were discussing.

"Good morning. Glad you decided to stop by and see the rescue." Christie held out her hand for the woman, who wore a long prairie dress with a cut-off denim jacket and a pair of pointed suede boots with spike heels. Not really popular footwear for touring around horses.

Abby spied Christie glancing at her footwear. "I have other flat boots in my vehicle if I need to grab them. I had a meeting out and thought I'd head over on the way back."

"I can take you through the primary areas, but if you want to see the horses and the corrals, the other boots would be better. Not only for ensuring you don't ruin the boots you're wearing, but also for safety. You want to move quickly in case a horse steps back or something and your foot's in the way."

"Sounds like a woman of experience."

"Yep, nothing like having a horse back onto your foot. I wear steel toes now and so do the volunteers working with the horses. Never had an accident yet, but better to be safe than sorry."

"Makes sense. Listen, I hope it's okay that I popped in without an appointment."

Christie glanced over to Rene who was moving back and forth on her feet, eager to return to what she'd been doing. "All good. Thanks Rene. I'll take it from here."

Rene addressed Abby as she walked away. "Nice meeting you."

"You too."

Christie smiled as Abby turned back to face her. "Are you here for a short tour or--?"

"I can't do a real long tour, but yes, that would be nice." She returned Christie's smile but appeared fidgety. "Listen, about the other day. We've been having one thing happen after another. I think Dax had simply reached the end of his rope with the last issue."

"All good. No need to explain. I know how that goes. When things are going well, you have to not go off wondering what's going to occur to ruin it."

"I heard some of what happened here last year with someone dying after an accident. Has it caused a lot of problems for the nonprofit?"

Christie led Abby toward the door that would take them over to the main horse barn. "It wasn't fun, that's for sure. But we weathered it. We have some new people on board and even with everything going nuts for a while, we still had a wonderful fundraiser."

"Good to hear."

"You want to change your boots before we

head over, or do you want to stick to the main areas?"

"If you don't mind, I think I will change these boots. She hit the key fob on a set of keys she retrieved from her purse, then headed toward a white Range Rover.

Christie waited until Abby had changed her footwear and then waved toward the primary work barn. Abby followed behind Christie, who pointed to some of the pregnant mares in the corral before entering the large barn, which was a hub of activity with people coming and going.

"As you can see, we rely heavily on volunteers. We show our appreciation for their work by providing some basic wellness checkups for their own horses and some discounts on any animal or farm products they purchase through the rescue. Our vet, Lana, is in charge of this area."

Christie ticked off with her fingers as she continued, "We have basically three primary areas in the rescue. First, there's the recovery and respite for neglected horses, ones that are here for vet care that are pay for service donors. They board here instead of at home as it's easier to keep an eye on them for any changes and the vets like having to only come here instead of driving out to ranches. Which also helps the horse's owner too since they don't need to be on site. The boarding is incorporated into the vet's fee."

"That sounds like a great way to manage it."

Christie beamed at the praise. "It really is. We contacted vets to find out what issues they had, as well as ranchers, and this has helped them out. We even pick up the animals if needed to bring them here."

"I thought I had a great business sense, but you all really have your act together. Do you have a degree in business or economics?"

Christie shook her head. "Nope. Actually, my background is in nursing. But I quit that after I moved her to be closer to my pop when he was recovering from an injury."

Abby's expression crumpled. "Oh, I hope he's okay. My folks are getting older, and I worry about them all the time. I wish I could get them to move here but they say they're too settled in with their friends."

"Good friends are hard to find so I don't blame them. But to answer your question, yes. All good now with him." Christie changed the subject. There was a fine line between getting too friendly with a potential donor about personal or private matters. She continued, "Anyway, still learning. And we have an exceptional team of staff and board members."

Abby nodded. "What's the third thing you do here?"

"Oh, almost forgot. This is what we're really proud of. We supply equine therapy for disabled individuals and veterans."

Abby's eyes flickered with excitement. "Really? That would be so good, um, sorry. I didn't mean to interrupt you. Please continue."

"No worries. Often they work with horses that have also experienced some trauma, so it's a win-win. And the program for the disabled helps with lots of various things, like balance for instance. I'd have to get one of the team to give you more of the details about that if you're interested."

"Wow. I didn't realize you did so much here. I'm really impressed."

"Thanks. It took a lot of figuring out the best way forward, but it's a nice combination as we have income from the vet services and some of the therapy that goes to pay for those areas not covered by our generous donors."

Christie stepped over to a stall where a handsome gelding appeared in the door opening. "This is Fred. His owner had health issues and wasn't able to care for Fred, so he asked us to take him. Fred's already getting better. Aren't you, Fred?" The horse neighed and bobbed his head.

Abby chuckled. "That's so funny. It's like he's agreeing with you."

"More like he knows I'll usually give him a treat."

She reached over to a nearby bucket and retrieved a long carrot from a mix of carrots and apples. "Would you like to give it to him?"

"Sure." She took the carrot from Christie and as she raised her arm, her sleeve fell back to her elbow. Abby's arm appeared even more black and blue. She caught Christie eying the bruises. "It's not what you think."

"Abby, you can speak freely with me. It won't go any further. But do you need help?"

She lowered her gaze and shook her head. When she met Christie's stare again, tears had gathered in her eyes. "I...don't want to talk about it."

Christie exhaled. "Okay, but please know that I'm here if you require anything. You just call on me if you need me."

"Thanks. I can see that you would have been a great nurse. You have a compassionate spirit about you. And I will take you up on that offer if I need it. I appreciate your saying that. It's a comfort." She wiped her eyes. "Now, is there anything else I should see of the operations?"

Christie replied, "Let's go back into the main building." They walked in silence back to the adjoining barn, which housed the offices. "This is where we do much of the nonprofit's administrative items, the main area on the ground floor is used for lunches and we rent it out for community events. We have an apartment up on that side of the barn where we have our security stay during the evening hours. And in the far back, we keep some of our hay and other items that need protection from the elements."

"Very nice. Everything is organized very well."

"Would you like something to drink?" Christie asked.

"Sure. Do you have coffee?"

"Are Texans proud of our state?"

Abby laughed. "I'm going to take that as a big yes."

"Yeppers. Follow me and we'll go up to the conference room upstairs."

They mounted the stairs and once in the breakroom, Christie nodded to the coffee pot. "Rene just made a fresh pot just before you arrived, so should still be good. Do you take cream? Sugar?"

"Just cream. Thanks."

Abby accepted the mug handed to her and poured the offered cream into her cup. "Are you having any?"

"I've already had three cups and if I have another, I'll be swinging from the chandelier. That is, if we had one."

Christie motioned to a nearby lounge chair before taking the one opposite. "Is there anything else that you'd like to know about the rescue?"

"I'm, um, we're considering holding an open house during our grand opening. Would there be a way to partner with the rescue so that we could help the group at the same time?"

Christie chose her words carefully. "I'd have to get approval from the board. In theory, it sounds great. However,...I'm just going to be honest here...there may be some pushback."

"Really? Why?" Abby took a sip of her coffee.

"Because you're a winery. We have some people on the board that may not be keen to associating the rescue with alcohol."

"Seriously?"

"Yes. Seriously. I know of at least three on the board that are teetotalers."

The woman cocked her head and her eyebrows knit together. "Nothing? Not even wine?"

Christie realized she'd crossed into murky waters and needed to get the conversation back on track. "I'm just saying that I'd need to get the board to approve it. That would be the same as with any other group, too, not just yours. If you send me the information, I'd be happy to share it at our upcoming board meeting."

Abby set down her cup. "That would be fantastic." She reached for her bag, but as she lifted it from the floor where she'd placed it, the contents spilled out. "Oh, great."

Christie helped her pick up some hand lotion, a couple of lipsticks, and her phone, along with crumpled receipts, handing them to Abby, who'd retrieved a container of dental floss and her wallet. "Thanks. Sorry. Clumsy of me."

Christie watched as Abby placed the items back in her purse. Was Abby normally self-effacing or was the woman anxious about something? Christie scanned the floor. "I think that's everything."

"Thanks. Anyway, I appreciate your speaking

to the board as I hope we can work together in a way that's mutually beneficial to both of us. Until then, I'd like to give a donation. I just need to know the name for the check. It's Horse Haven, correct?"

"Yes. You're correct."

Christie watched as Abby wrote in the name on the check. She stood and smiled, "Christie, thanks for showing me around and thank you for your kind offer."

"Happy to help. Let me see you downstairs."

Abby handed the check to Christie, who walked her out of the room.

"I can make it from here. Thanks again." Abby stuck out her hand as the two women parted and they shook hands.

Christie watched as Abby made her way out of the open doorway. After she'd had exited, Christie glimpsed down at the check.

One hundred and fifty thousand dollars.

Whoa. If only every major donation was as easy. Bryson hadn't been kidding that they would provide a large check. Christie would want to leave a bit early to get this check along with the regular deposit into the bank today. Returning to her office, she placed the large contribution in the zippered bag with the other donations for the day. This afternoon when her accounting staff came in, all the donations would be tallied, and receipts sent along with thank you cards to all the donors.

After placing the deposit bag in a locked desk drawer, Christie sat back down at her desk, browsing through emails that had come in while she was giving Abby the tour. She gathered the donation paperwork, deciding to work on it tomorrow when her mind was fresh, and she could think about some ways to incorporate the recent contribution. She was making progress on all the messages on the computer and had just hit send on her latest email when Rene buzzed her office.

Rene said it was Abby. "She really sounds upset."

Oh shoot. Maybe she had goofed on the check. As she thanked Rene and picked up the phone's receiver, Christie glanced at the time on her computer. Abby hadn't been gone long. Maybe forty-five minutes to an hour at the most. She answered her phone. "This is Christie."

Abby's voice was strained as she cried out, "I'm going to take you up on your offer to help me. Dax is dead."

CHAPTER FIVE

Christie could barely respond as Abby launched into how she'd returned to a quiet facility. The words came out in a torrent as Christie listened.

"I came in and called out, but there was no response. The crew left for lunch, and they weren't expected back together so we could have a longer workday tomorrow. Dax hadn't wanted to stop moving forward on the production. He said he wanted to work through today as well to get things ready for tomorrow, which is why I came over there first. I thought he might want to go grab something to eat. But I couldn't find Dax. His truck was here, so I knew he hadn't gone home."

There was silence on the line before Abby continued.

"I don't know why, but I went up the stairs at the older vat in the back ... and that's when I found him. I don't know if he fell or ..." Abby broke off sobbing.

"Have you called the sheriff?"

She sputtered. "No. I, I didn't know what to do. I'm the only one here. You know how they are. They always suspect the spouse first. Christie, I'm scared. I never laid a hand on Dax. Believe me."

A shiver went up Christie's spine, and she realized she was clutching the phone tightly. She relaxed her grip. Why would Abby say such a thing to her?

Abby continued, "You know that I was with you. There's no way I could have done this. Please help me!"

Christie's mind raced. "Don't touch anything. You need to call the sheriff's office. I'll be there shortly."

There was silence on the line. "Abby, you there?"

"Yes, I don't feel well. I think I may be sick."

"Sit down and put your head between your knees. You've had a big shock."

Abby moaned. "Okay."

Christie could hear the woman's labored

breathing. "Listen, is this your cell phone number?" She bolted from her chair, pulling her jacket from the back of her door. Before putting the phone on speaker, she changed hands grabbing her purse, and keys. "Abby, you still there?"

Abby squeaked out between her sobbing. "Yes."

"Okay, give me the number so I can call you back on my mobile."

"Please don't hang up. I'm scared."

"Abby, are you sure you're alone?"

"I... I think so. I don't know." Her moans grew louder.

"Listen, get into your office or your SUV and lock the doors. Can you do that?"

"Yes, I believe so."

"Okay, I'm going to stay on the line with you until you do it. Go now."

Christie could hear the woman's boots jogging across the concrete floor and her labored breathing.

"Did you make it to the office?"

No response.

Christie heard a car's lock pinging. "Okay, you're in your vehicle?"

"Yes. I didn't want to stay in there." Abby broke down crying again. "What will I do now?"

Christie quickly typed out an email message to Rene about calling the sheriff's office. The woman raced into her office and Christie pointed to the phone. Christie jotted a quick note that she'd be leaving. Rene, whose demeanor, and facial expression relayed her shock at the situation, bobbed her head.

"Fine, that's good. Now lock your doors and hang up. I'll call you with my mobile. Here I'm calling right now. The call dropped and Abby had picked up Christie's call on her mobile.

"Christie, are you there?"

"Yes, I'm here."

"I'm sorry. I didn't know who else to call."

"It's okay. Rene called the sheriff's office for you and I'm heading out now."

"Thank you. I don't know what I'm going to do." The woman's anguished cries traveled over the phone.

"Don't worry. It'll be all right." Christie locked her office door behind her before rushing down the stairs to her truck, continuing to deliver soothing words of comfort to Abby.

"Abby, I'm leaving now. I'll be there as soon as I can. Keep taking slow, deep breaths."

In her truck, Christie noted that she'd be switching her phone to her vehicle in case they got disconnected. All she heard was Abby muttering softly to herself. "I didn't think he'd do it." She repeated it.

Was Abby talking about Dax? Or someone else? Do what? Surely Dax hadn't seemed like a person who might harm himself.

Christie shoved the truck in gear, steeling herself for whatever she would face when she arrived.

~

The winery was already in an uproar of people coming and going when Christie arrived. She didn't know if they would even allow her to be with Abby if they were already questioning her.

The line had gone dead when she drove into the gravel lot, suggesting that Abby or someone else had disconnected the call.

She made to exit her truck when a deputy came up to her window. She rolled it down as he approached.

"Ma'am, you can't come in here. You'll need to leave." He gestured back toward the road.

"Hello Deputy. My name's Christie Taylor and..."

"You're Pop's daughter?"

"Yes. Um, anyway—"

"Great guy. What a sense of humor. He always has us laughing."

She nodded. "Yes, anyway, I'm here because Abby called me."

"She called you?"

His eyes were hidden by his aviator sunglasses, but she noticed the tone of his voice had returned to professional mode. "When was this?"

"When she found Dax. My office assistant made the call to you."

"Step out of the vehicle." He grasped her door handle as Christie exited. "I'm fairly sure we'll need to get a statement from you on the time and what was said. Follow me."

Christie walked behind the man, watching as a crime investigation crew began donning their gear. Certainly, it didn't mean foul play, but was simply a matter of protocol, but she shivered all the same.

Christie was led into the vast warehouse where various men and women in differing agency uniforms stood at the back. The deputy stepped in front of her, blocking Christie's view. He opened a door into an office where Abby sat opposite the sheriff and a woman Christie didn't recognize.

The sheriff stood. "Ms. Taylor, come in." He waved to a chair close to Abby.

"Ms. Calhan was telling us that as soon as she found Mr. Calhan, she contacted you."

"Yes, that's correct."

"She also states that she was at the rescue this morning, leaving about an hour and a half or more before she called you."

Christie nodded before replying, "Yes."

"Ms. Frank, would you please stay with Mrs. Calhan while I speak with Ms. Taylor?"

Abby grabbed Christie's hand. "Please don't leave. I'm afraid."

The sheriff spoke, "Mrs. Calhan, Ms. Frank will stay with you. She can get you something to drink if that would help."

He motioned for Christie to exit the room. Once they were away from the door, he opened his notepad. "Okay, Christie. You sure get yourself into these things. How are you involved this time?"

"Look, I can't help it that people die."

"True. But they sure seem to have that happen a lot when you're around." He winked but Christie didn't enjoy his teasing. She gave him an overview of Abby calling her at the rescue.

He scribbled some notes. "If you'll let me know the time Mrs. Calhan arrived this morning and a general rundown of your visit."

Christie went through the events of the

morning, thinking back to recall the time that Abby had arrived.

"And how did she seem?"

"I'm not sure what you mean."

"How was she acting?"

Christie thought back to the morning. Abby had appeared a bit anxious or jumpy, but she didn't know her well enough to know if this differed from her normal behavior. "I think she may have been a bit preoccupied, but nothing that I saw seemed out of the ordinary."

He nodded. "Anything happen while she was with you?"

Christie thought back to their conversation about the bruises. If she shared about that, would it point the finger toward Abby and give her motive if it turned out to be more than an accident? No, there wasn't time for her to come back to the winery and kill Dax. Was there? Plus, Abby was adamant that she had received the bruising while doing work, yet she also didn't want to talk about it. Maybe she'd felt embarrassed that Christie thought it was due to abuse. Either that or she was covering up for Dax.

The sheriff stared at her, waiting for her to answer. "I can't recall anything that would be out of the ordinary. I've only chatted with her a few times."

"Besides today?"

Christie nodded. "Yes, I came over here and she gave me a tour. I'd left when one of the crew had an accident."

"Oh, yes. I heard about that. A Cal Weiss. I believe he fell on some metal steps and hit his head on a metal railing."

"Wait. Why would you know about an accident here?"

He lowered his voice. "From what I understand, there was some altercation between Mr. Weiss and Mr. Calhan. That's what someone who didn't want to be named said. However, Mr. Weiss said he'd fallen and hit his head. So, no charges."

"Do you think that's what happened to Dax Calhan? He fell and hit his head?"

"I can't speculate on anything in the

investigation."

"Oh, right. I wonder if he hit his head, then got up and fell backwards down the stairs. Wait, then Abby would have seen him right away when she came into the facility."

Her eyes grew wide. "Oh my gosh, he fell into the vat and drowned?"

The sheriff chuckled and shook his head. "You sure you don't want to become a detective? That mind goes from zero to ninety miles an hour."

"Can you at least let me know if he was found in the vat of wine?"

He scrunched up his mouth. Even without saying a word, she'd gotten her answer.

"If he fell into the vat, unless he was unconscious, he would have been able to climb out. And Abby's a little woman. No way she could have pushed him in and then kept him from saving himself. She didn't do it." She took a deep breath of relief, realizing that she had wanted some proof to convince herself of Abby's innocence.

"Right now, until we find out more about

what happened, we're going to keep things close so no going off and sharing anything."

Christie nodded. "Okay, sure."

"Even speculation." He cocked his head toward her, a look of admonition on his face.

She grinned and made the sign of crossing her heart. "Absolutely."

"I know where to contact you if I need you, so you're free to go."

"But Abby asked me—"

"Goodbye Ms. Taylor." The sheriff was back in professional mode.

Christie hated that she'd been dismissed so casually. But truth be told, she didn't really know Abby or Dax. It would be better if she stayed out of it like the sheriff had said. She shot off a text even though she was pretty sure they'd taken Abby's phone.

> Had to leave. Won't let me talk to
>
> you. If need me, contact me.

She put her phone on the console and backed away from the winery entrance but not leaving yet. Something Abby had said kept tickling at the edge of her mind. What was it?

Finally, she realized what it was. Abby had said the words, "There's no way I could have done this." Yet, she hadn't said 'there's no way I *would* have done this.' A simple distinction in wording, but it made a significant difference in perception.

Was Abby telling the truth or had she been planting the thought of innocence in Christie's mind? She grit her teeth together. Had Abby decided to use Christie as an unsuspecting alibi to murder?

CHAPTER SIX

Christie wondered what she should do next. Should she share this information? It didn't mean anything except to her. She certainly couldn't tell the sheriff that Abby had used the word, could versus would. He'd look at her like she'd lost her marbles. She was making too much out of a simple choice of words. But she knew—words matter.

It was a bit like when a ballot measure would say something like taxes would probably not go up. That simple word—probably—pretty much guaranteed taxes would go up. The power of a simple word to manipulate people was something Christie had discovered in the last few years. Especially as she'd collected some fundraising communications from other groups. Now that she knew some tricks that marketers and politicians used, she noticed them a lot quicker. Which was probably why Abby's statement had wiggled its way into her conscious mind. Simple choices of words matter.

But she also needed to consider the facts. Abby had been at the rescue for quite some time. If she had killed her husband, she would have had to do it before she left to come to Horse Haven. Yet that made no sense. They could certainly figure out the timeline. Plus, she couldn't see a petite woman like Abby being able to get Dax up those stairs and into the vat. If he'd been alive, he'd have grabbed for her if they'd fought, and she'd have also gone into the vat. No, it made no sense.

She thought back to the last few days. While she'd only seen Dax when he burst into the office, Bryson tended to think that Dax was more bark than bite. If that were true, it was most likely a terrible accident. Trying to do something quickly and either lost his footing or hit his head, causing his death.

Her phone's ring broke her reverie. It was Lana.

"Hey, just heard. You all right?"

"Yes, Abby called me when she found her husband, but they're not allowing anyone to speak with her. I only got in a few words before they escorted me out."

"What a terrible tragedy. Any thoughts on what happened?"

"No, and they wouldn't give out any information. But I'm thinking he must have fallen into the vat and drown."

"Oh, how horrible."

"Yes, though I think he would have to have been unconscious or something else. I didn't think to ask if he had any health issues. Maybe he had a heart attack or something like that. From what I've learned about him, he was a very Type A personality and was intent on getting the winery ready to open."

"Could be. Listen, are you still there?"

"Yes. I pulled over in their parking lot to wrap my head around everything and allow my adrenaline to settle down. Why?"

"I think I'm going to need some help with a mare out here at the Russell's place. Since you're already out this way, could you come over?"

"Yes. I can be there soon." She gasped.

"What is it?"

"They just brought out the body."

"Poor guy. Curtis is going to be so upset. I'm sure Dax will be missed."

"What? Did Curtis know him?" Christie asked.

"Yep. Pop knew him too."

Christie watched as the techs loaded the van and then shut the doors. She should be used to that sight, but knowing a life was gone was always traumatic. "Did you meet or know him then?"

"Not well, but he'd helped with some stuff around the place, and like I said, Curtis knows, I mean, knew him."

"Really? He helped out at the house. I would think he'd have been busy with the winery and wouldn't have any time for anything else. I'll need to ask Curtis about him. The only time I saw him, he was yelling at Abby." She refrained from saying anything about the young woman's bruises.

"Hmm. I don't know, but you could ask Curtis

what he thinks. I'm going to let you go. See you in a bit."

The call ended.

Christie started the truck and then a thought came to her. She made a quick call to the rescue.

Rene answered the phone in her cheerful voice. "Horse Haven. How may I help you?"

"Hey Rene, it's Christie. Has the deposits been done yet?"

"No. I'm waiting for Lori to arrive. What do you need?"

"Go into the bag and remove the check from Abby Calhan. We're going to hold off on depositing it until I'm sure that Abby is still good with that size donation."

"I'll go do it right now."

"Thanks. Also, as a heads-up, I'm going out to the Russell's to help Lana out with a sick mare. So not sure when I'll be back. If you need me, call. Otherwise, I'll see you tomorrow."

"Will do. Another call coming in. Bye!"

Christie started up the truck and slowly backed away from the emergency vehicles. She did a three-point turn and made her way down the long driveway, turning right onto the main road. She hadn't gone far when she noticed two trucks stopped in a gravel pull-off by a bank of mailboxes. As she drove by, the man in the truck turned his head, the large white bandage he bore let her immediately know it was Cal. The other man, older with a gray beard and a worn ball cap, glanced her way, but Christie didn't recognize him. As she passed Cal's truck, she spied a logo with a ram's head on the door of the second truck with a brand on top.

She struggled to think where she'd seen that logo. Topping the next hill, the pair of trucks disappeared from her view. But in the distance, she could see a large metal gate across the next drive. At the crossbar along the top, the same brand was displayed. It was the neighbor that was in litigation with Dax and Abby.

Was Cal telling him about what had happened to Dax? Christie thought hard. Had Cal been there when the accident occurred? Abby said everyone had left for the day. If so, unless he'd been called, he wouldn't know about Dax's death. Which meant that he was possibly feeding some information about the winery's processes. But it was a strange coincidence that he'd be talking to the neighbor right after they found Dax. Had one of these men been at the winery when Dax died?

She'd need to find out what really happened with Cal's accident. It was awfully convenient that two accidents had occurred so close to each other. Had it been a fight between the two men, or were they both accidents? Abby had said some things were happening that were causing issues at the winery. If that were the case, had Cal been sabotaging the efforts of the winery on behalf of the neighbor? If so, for what reason?

~

The smell of coffee brewing met Christie as she entered Pop's kitchen. Curtis was sitting there, a peach kolache in his hand. "Morning Chrissie." He nodded before taking a bite of the pastry.

"Morning Curtis." She went over and placed a quick kiss on the top of his balding, grey head.

"Morning Pop." She kissed his grizzled cheek.

"Morning, darlin. Coffee?" He pointed to the pot which was beeping to signal it was ready for pouring.

She nodded. "That would be great."

"Grab you a kolache."

She shook her head, "I'll pass."

"Since when?"

"Since my jeans have gotten snug."

"It's pretty normal to gain some weight as you age." He handed her the steaming cup of coffee.

"Oh, great. Not only am I getting fat, but old too."

"Hogwash." Curtis wiped his mustache and beard of any crumbs. "You're just fine as ya are."

"Thanks Curtis." She took a sip of the coffee, waiting for Pop to join them before she asked her question.

"What's on your mind? You said you had some questions for me."

"Yes. You've most likely heard that Dax Calhan died."

Curtis shook his head. "Such a dang shame.

Young fella like that. His business set to take off, pretty young wife. Terrible, just terrible."

"What did you think of Dax?"

He brushed pastry crumbs from his beard. "What do ya mean?"

Christie didn't want to put any thoughts in his mind. "You know, personality-wise."

"Ah, gotcha. Great guy. Would give you the shirt off his back. Funny sense of humor. You should have met him. You'd have liked him."

Christie's brows knit together. This was a far cry from the man she'd seen at the winery. "Actually, I sort of met him. But he was in a foul mood, yelling at his wife. He didn't even acknowledge my presence or apologize."

"Hmm. That doesn't seem like him. But I can't say I've known him that long, but he's always been nice to me and the other guys. Respectful too."

"Curtis, do you think, um, do you think he could be the type of person to get physical with his wife?"

"Whatever do ya mean?"

"You know, maybe when he gets angry or drinks?"

"No. No way. What would make you think such a thing?"

"I saw lots of bruising on Abby's arms, and he was yelling at her when I saw him."

Curtis pushed back in his chair and folded his arms across his chest. "Well, I certainly never seen him with his wife, but that don't sound like him at all. Plus, he don't drink."

"What do you mean? He's running a winery."

"Some guys offered him a beer and he wouldn't even have one. Nope, can't see him as someone who would get smashed."

"Did you ever meet Abby?"

"Who?" Curtis asked.

"Dax's wife."

"Nope, can't say I did."

Christie looked longingly at the kolaches. Maybe half of one would be okay she reasoned before turning her focus back to Curtis. "How did you meet Dax?"

Pop refilled the cups with coffee.

"Ah, he came into the veteran's group."

"He was a veteran?"

"Yep. Two tours. But then he chose to get out because of his situation."

"What situation?"

"Diabetes. He found out during the second tour. I think he said he ended up in the hospital one time. He tried to manage it but, well, he wouldn't go into it much. But that's why he stays away from drinking. Messed too much with his blood sugar, among other reasons. But that's not for me to say."

Christie's background in nursing went into overdrive. It wasn't unusual for diabetics who hadn't gotten their blood sugar stabilized to have wild mood swings. That was why Dax was so different, depending on the situation. And if he'd had some blood sugar issue when he climbed up to the vat, it could account for his death. It made sense, as he was certainly strong enough to pull himself out of the vat, even if only to hold on until someone heard him call for help.

Though if everyone were gone and his blood

sugar decreased, that could have had a factor in his fall. This would be good news for Abby, as she was with Christie, and it would be important to find out if he'd had low blood sugar issues.

The funeral was bound to be scheduled soon, so maybe she'd have time to speak with Abby about it then. Plus, she may be able to find out what the autopsy report showed once it was completed. It was looking more like it was just a tragic accident, after all.

"Christie?"

"Oh, yes, Pop?" She smiled at her father, who had a look of concern on his face. "Are you okay?"

"Yes, I'm good. I was just thinking about everything."

"Well, let's talk about something else less depressing. Like weddings instead of funerals."

"Pop, enough. I've already told you that when I get ready, you'll be the first to know."

"I ain't getting no younger."

Christie stood and took her cup to the sink. "Maybe. But you are getting more ornery."

"Me? Never." He winked.

Christie said goodbye to the pair and struck out for her house. She'd walked over and her boots crunched the gravel underneath her feet as she made her way home. She was relieved that Dax's death looked to be an accident. Though two things kept swimming to the surface of her conscious mind.

First, what was Cal doing talking to the person in litigation with the Calhan's and second, Dax's words.

"What have you done?"

CHAPTER SEVEN

The day of the funeral, Christie laid out her dress along with a jacket. There would be a service at the Fort Sam Houston military gravesite. Bryson, Pop, Curtis, and Christie were all riding together into San Antonio.

As they arrived, they made their way towards an area at the back. The rows of white headstones of those who had served their country or died defending its freedom were a somber reminder of the cost of liberty. Bryson pulled up behind another vehicle and they merged with others, headed toward the small canopy with a smattering of chairs.

Christie spied Abby in the front, weeping softly with an older woman wearing large sunglasses and a hat with a large brim, embracing her in a side hug. On the other side of Abby, another older couple, a younger woman, and a clean-shaven man sat with grief etched on their faces. This must be Dax's parents and siblings.

As they took their places toward the back of the group, the pastor began speaking. When he finished, the honor guard took their positions and fired their guns three times. When the sound of taps began, Christie felt the tears spring to her eyes. She noted that her father and Curtis were overcome with emotion as well, both having served at some point in their lives.

After the service and the group had dispersed, Christie went up to Abby who stood next to the couple. The woman who'd been consoling Abby was speaking to the soldiers. "I'm so sorry, Abby. Please accept my condolences. And if there's anything you need, don't hesitate to ask."

Abby wiped her nose with her handkerchief. "Thanks, Christie. Could you come by later this week? I need some time to process everything."

"Certainly. We can set something up when you're ready." Christie started to say that she'd held onto the check, but it simply wasn't the right time for it. She went over to where Pop and Curtis were talking to some other people she didn't know. One she recognized. It was Cal. Maybe these were the work crew of the winery. As she approached, Cal blurted goodbye to the others and strode off.

"Hmm, did I do something?" Christie asked.

"No. He was already leaving when you came over." Pop wiped his brow. "I'm ready for some grub. How 'bout ya'll?"

Bryson nodded. "I'm with you. What are you in the mood for?"

Christie laughed. "You should know these two by now. Tip Top Café and chicken-fried steak sound good?"

Pop and Curtis agreed with a hearty, "What are we waiting for?"

After lunch at the café, they drove back to Comfort and Bryson dropped off Curtis before taking Pop home. Pop waved goodbye to them, going inside to watch television while he snoozed. Bryson pulled up at Christie's house.

"What are you doing the rest of the afternoon?"

"Probably get ready for next week. How about

you?"

"Turns out I'm going to be saying goodbye to my dogs."

"Oh, no. Why?"

"Well, they are trained to serve. Without it and me being gone so much of the day, it's not fair to them. I tried giving them lots of exercise before I leave in the mornings and when I get home, but it's really not enough. They are working dogs. They need lots of activity and sadly, I'm not able to give it to them no matter how hard I try. I told my friend about it and now they're going to live where they can put their talents to use. I guess even dogs have a hard time retiring."

Christie nodded. "Interesting point. Do you think Dax struggled after he had to leave the service? It could account for his driven personality to see things accomplished efficiently with no errors."

Bryson shrugged his shoulders. "Who knows? The winery and all the work there gave him the purpose he needed."

"Do you think it was going to be successful?

They certainly had the money. Which brings up another point. Where did they get the money?"

"Are we going to keep talking out here or are you going to invite me up to your house?"

"I think here is better." It's not that she didn't want to invite Bryson in, but she really wanted some alone time to recharge after a busy week.

He sighed. "Okay. Well, what I learned from snippets of conversation is that the money was Abby's."

"Oh? Where did she get her money?"

"Now, don't get ideas in your head when I tell you."

"What do you mean? What sort of ideas?"

"It was a large insurance settlement. After her first husband died."

Christie was taken aback at this information. "Okay, you did that on purpose. As you know, I'm going to want to hear more about it. Come on up."

Bryson followed Christie up the stairs. "Do you want some coffee?"

"Pie?" He asked.

"Sorry, I gave the rest of the pie to Pop so I

wouldn't be tempted having it in the house and I haven't made anything sweet since." She opened her door and walked over to hang up her jacket.

"Shoot. Okay, coffee will have to do." He moved over to add water to the coffeepot's reservoir while Christie pulled the container of coffee from a nearby cabinet, measuring the scoops into the filter basket of the coffeemaker. Once the coffee was going, Christie shucked off her flats, before taking a seat on the sofa, pulling a soft comforter over her.

"Want me to start a fire in the woodstove?"

"That would be lovely. It's got enough nip in the air that it would get rid of some of that cold from the humidity in here."

She watched as Bryson pulled some kindling from a bucket next to the stove, then threw back the cover when the coffee beeped it was ready.

As she poured coffee for them both, she heard the warming sound of the kindling crackling as the fire took hold. He set a larger log toward the back and moved aside to wait for the fire to get going well before he turned away.

"Here you go, I added some whipped cream on top and some chocolate sprinkles. That's about all the dessert items I have right now."

"I'll take it." He took a sip, licking his top lip from the cream.

She burrowed back under the covers as he added another log to the blazing fire and closed the glass front. "That's nice. Thanks."

"You're welcome." He moved to the end of the couch, where he set down his cup. "Foot rub?"

Christie responded enthusiastically, "Oh, yes. You don't even have to ask." She moved to place a pillow behind her back against the sofa's large arm as Bryson took one of her stocking feet in his warm hands. As he began massaging her feet, Christie sighed with delight. "Okay, I'm putting this at the top of my acts of service list."

"Noted. I just know that you were on your feet a lot with the animals this week more than usual."

"True. That's really feels nice. Now tell me more about Abby and the first husband."

Bryson held up a finger. "Hold on." He took a swig of coffee before continuing to knead the ball of her foot. "Dax told me about it. I don't even know what brought it up, but Abby was married fairly young to an older guy. Pretty wealthy from what it sounds like. He piloted his own plane."

"Oh no. Did it crash?"

"Now, you're getting ahead of the story. Other foot please."

Christie pulled her foot back under the blanket while Bryson massaged her right foot.

"Okay, sorry." She sipped at the coffee, wishing she'd added some of the chocolate sprinkles to her cup.

Bryson continued. "No, not the plane. His car. Brakes failed or something."

"Hmm. That would be pretty easy to see if someone tampered with them."

"True. And he was driving Abby's car, not his own."

He patted her foot that he was done. "Thanks for the foot rub. That was delightful."

"You're welcome." He picked up his coffee, staring into the fire.

"So, he died and left Abby with money?"

"Not just money. We're talking major money."

"That means it's most likely that the donation she gave us was her money, then?"

He nodded. "Probably. I know she had the money to invest in the winery. Though if it doesn't do well, they could stand to lose thousands."

Christie pulled her knees up close to her. "But it means that it takes a big motive out of the way if she was the one with the money." She picked at a piece of lint on the blanket. "Who was that lady sitting next to her at the funeral?"

"I'm not one hundred percent sure, but I believe that's the sister of the first husband."

Christie knit her brow together. "That seems a bit strange, doesn't it?"

"Abby really doesn't have much family left, just her parents and they weren't able to come as her dad is ill. From what I gather, Abby and the sister were pretty close and still are. I don't have any proof, but I'd bet that Abby gives her money." He rose and grabbed another log, which he added to the fire.

Christie repositioned herself so she could see the fire better. "That's interesting. I wonder if she inherits Abby's money if she dies?"

Bryson chuckled. "You and your mind. Constantly thinking of crazy ideas."

"It's not crazy. If the sister were to inherit Abby's money, that could give her motive." She crossed her arms.

"Motive to kill Dax?"

"Um, I guess not. But what if Abby had told her Dax was abusing her?"

"Are you kidding me? Did you see that woman? She looked like she wouldn't hurt a fly."

Christie pointed her finger at him. "Looks can be deceiving. What if they were both in on it to get rid of Dax?"

Bryson sighed. "Seriously?"

Christie burst out laughing. "Okay, wild goose chase."

"More like wild horses chase."

She smiled. "Speaking of horses, up for a ride tomorrow afternoon?"

"Sure. Now come here."

Christie snuggled her back up against Bryson as they watched the flames licking the logs in the woodstove. She sighed with contentment, knowing that they didn't need to speak to be perfectly content in each other's company. She felt her breath slow as she dozed in his arms. When she woke later, she was stretched out on the couch and Bryson had left. The fire had burned down to orange coals, so she stoked it back up before adding more wood. She cuddled back on the couch, and as she watched the flames, she yawned. Her eyes grew heavy again as she lost herself to sleep.

CHAPTER EIGHT

Christie was talking to Lana on the cell phone when she shared what Bryson had told her. "Abby's first husband died."

Lana responded. "Okay, that seems weird to have two husbands die in accidents. But it doesn't mean she killed them. She'd have to be really confident about doing that and not think she'd get caught."

"It's certainly interesting at any rate. I'd really like to find out if it's true she received a large insurance settlement. Though it was had been suspicious, I'm sure that it would have been looked into. But it makes me wonder if Dax also had a large insurance policy. Who knows? Maybe the money's running low and she wanted more. Greed can be a powerful motive." Christie stretched her back. The couch may have been comfy while she'd been napping, but she was now stiff from it.

"What else did Bryson say?"

"Not much. He'd lit a fire in the woodstove, and I fell asleep. I'm not normally one for naps, but I guess I needed it."

Lana replied, "A nap sounds appealing with the chill in the air. Since you're going to be out riding with Bryson tomorrow, rain check on hanging out?"

Christie thought about it. "Sure. We could go to a new movie at the Forum or grab some dinner."

"Sounds good. What are you doing with the rest of your day?" Lana asked.

"I may bake a pie or two so I can send one over to the winery if you want to come over for dinner."

Lana groaned. "That sounds nice but can't tonight. Playing my role of chauffeur for the kids again."

"Okay, text me what show you want to see."

Lana said, "Will do."

Christie stared at her phone before calling Bryson.

He answered. "Hey there."

Christie tucked her hair behind her ear as she moved off the couch. "Hi. Sorry, I fell asleep on you. Looking into that fire must have made me sleepy."

"All good. I had to come back to get the dogs ready to go or I would have been right there with you."

"I'm surprised that I didn't even feel you move or hear you leave."

His deep, calming voice came through the phone. "That's what happens when you trust someone. I think even in your sleep you register their presence."

"That sounds a bit woo-woo but makes some sense. Anyway, I'm calling as I want to test out a new pie recipe and thought you might want dinner too."

"As long as there's pie, you know you can count on me. But what happened to no more pie?" Bryson chuckled.

"What's that admonition—all things in moderation? Well, today I think we can be less strict, but I'm still going to cut back on the junk."

"I'm with you. Since knowing you, I've noticed my clothes getting snug too. What time should I be there?"

"How about six or six thirty? Will that work with the dogs?"

"Yes. I'm getting them ready now. It's hard to let them go but I know it's what's best for them. See ya then."

"Love you." She answered as she caught herself, surprised at her statement. It had simply come out.

"Love you too."

The call ended. Christie set down the phone, staring off into space for a moment. She felt discombobulated after her nap, like she was still tired, and that was unusual for her. But to say she loved Bryson without even thinking about it, this was something new. She stretched her arms over her head, feeling positively decadent for taking a nap instead of working on something. Before she did anything she needed to change out of these crumpled clothes. Donning a pair of leggings and a long tunic, she felt much more comfortable.

After pulling on some fluffy socks, she stood and bent over at the waist and flexed her back and legs. She needed to regain some energy, so she didn't feel so out of it. As she moved into some other stretches, she considered what would be a good pie to make that everyone would like. She shuffled into the kitchen where she poured a glass of water, contemplating ideas.

While fall often was filled with pies of apple, cherry, pumpkin, or pecan, she was in the mood for something lighter. She sat at her kitchen table and paged through her folder of recipes, looking for inspiration, until her eyes landed on a chocolate pudding pie recipe. Yet, she knew some people weren't big on chocolate. She could change it up and make the pie with a nice vanilla pudding.

She rose from her chair and went to her fridge. She had the basics but was missing cream cheese. Maybe she could get Bryson to pick some up on the way back.

She texted him.

> Can you pick up a couple of boxes of
> cream cheese on your way back?

Sure. I forgot to ask when we were chatting. How was the nap?

Heavenly.

Good. Anything else?

Um, I was thinking taco salad if that works. Could use some more avocado.

Got it. If you think of anything else, let me know.

Will do.

Christie hesitated before adding on to the text.

I appreciate you.

Ah, you're making me blush.

The phone pinged again.

I appreciate you too.

Christie set her phone down on the table and went to the pantry to gather the ingredients to make the pie crust. As she dug in the fridge, she spied a bag of pecans. That would be good to add in some nuts. She threw the nuts into her food processor, chopping them into smaller chunks.

The butter she'd left out that morning was exactly right in texture for mixing in with the flour and brown sugar. She measured out the pecans. She'd need enough for two pies. There was a smidge over two cups, so she divided it into around three quarters for each pie. Better to have some left if she needed it.

Adding in the flour, she used a spatula to incorporate all the ingredients, finally adding the nuts.

She pressed the mixture into a pie pan and then repeated the process for the next pie.

Now to make the pudding. While the original Arkansas Possum Pie she'd found called for chocolate pudding, Christie decided she'd call hers a Texas Armadillo pie with vanilla pudding instead.

She set to work, whisking the milk with the sugar over low heat. Once she was done with it, she made up a batch of chocolate pudding, too. She stuck them in the fridge until Bryson came with the cream cheese.

Pulling her whipping cream container from

the cabinet, she added heavy whipping cream to it before she inserted a cartridge into the top. It was fun to feel the container turn cold in her hand as it turned it from liquid form into fluffy whipping cream. She removed the cartridge and, placing the top back on, put it in the fridge as well.

Since she had time, she might as well prep all the items for the taco salad. She cut up lettuce, tomatoes, and grated some cheddar cheese. Then she made a pico-de-gallo with more of the tomatoes, serranoes, onion, and cilantro. She finished it with a squeeze of lime juice and some garlic salt. Now all she'd have to do when Bryson arrived would be to cook the hamburger meat.

After washing up the dishes, Christie's mind wandered. How could she find out about Abby's first husband? Had Dax known about the insurance money? Or maybe he felt threatened that she held the purse strings and started lashing out physically. Yet not one person who actually knew him said he was that kind of guy.

Who was Dax really?

Certainly, people can act one way with

acquaintances and quite another with their spouse.

But that led to another question. Had Abby had enough and decided that she needed to get him out of her life? If so, she wouldn't want to give up half her money to him in a divorce. Yet, there was no way Abby could have done it because she was with Christie when it occurred.

Christie admonished herself aloud. "Oh, stop it!"

Not every single death was due to foul play or something sinister. Sadly, accidents happened all the time that caused someone to die and leave lots of unanswered questions. Christie knew she needed to let it go, but she had such a curious mind, letting it go was easier said than done.

While she waited for Bryson, she decided to do a bit of dusting and vacuuming. One thing that was nice about her little cob home, it was easy to keep clean. Once she was done, she decided on a quick shower and a change of clothes. She'd finished drying her hair when she heard the tap-tap of him rapping his knuckles on her front door.

"Hi you. Came a bit early. Hope that's okay." He handed her a bouquet of fall flowers. "A lady at the store made me get these for you."

"Did she? I'll have to thank her." She winked.

He walked over to the table, depositing the bags down on it. "I wasn't sure if you wanted the tub or bars of cream cheese, so I got both. I also got a bunch of avocadoes. I figure we could make some guac to go on the salad. And I wasn't sure if you had tortilla strips, so I got some too."

"Oh geez. I'd totally forgotten. Thanks!"

Bryson rolled up his sleeves before washing his hands in the sink. Christie watched him from the corner of her eye as he hummed a tune. In a rare rush of emotion, she wanted to go up behind him and put her arms around him. Instead, she pulled a vase from a cabinet for the flowers before heading over to add water to it. He swapped the taps to the cold setting while drying his hands.

"Thanks." She added the water and began cutting the stems off the flowers as he worked on the guacamole. Taking the flowers over to a nearby console table, she faced him.

"What's wrong with you?"

He looked up from the cutting board. "Excuse me? This is the way I always make guac."

Christie laughed. "Sorry, that came out wrong. I meant, what annoying habits do you have?"

He made a strange face at her question before bursting out in laughter.

"It may seem funny, but it's the little annoying things that can cause all kinds of issues in a relationship." She sat down and, taking a cube of avocado, popped it in her mouth before she continued. "You know, the thing is, people always talk about compatibility, but the fact is that's the easy part. What about the part where you do things that drive each other crazy?"

"Such as?"

"Well, chewing with your mouth open, for starters."

He pursed his lips. "I didn't know I did."

"No, not you. I'm just saying things that people do out of habit that drive someone else crazy."

He slipped the avocado into a bowl, squeezing a lemon on them before mixing it up. "I guess you find those things out over time. You're right, marriage, much less any relationship, isn't about the good. It's about being able to see the other person's flaws and love them despite those quirks." He began mashing the avocado with a fork.

Christie thought about what he'd said. "I guess that's true. Off the top of your head, what is something that drives you crazy?"

"Why? You want tips on how to achieve it?"

She chuckled. "No. Just curious of what one or two might be."

"Okay. One of my pet peeves is using a knife as a screwdriver."

"Seriously?"

"Yes, seriously. Use the right tool."

"But a knife is handy and does the same job."

"Hence, the first flaw you've shown me." He winked.

Christie stood and went to the cabinet. "Garlic salt?"

"Yep. And I'll dice up a couple of tomatoes too."

Christie set the container down. "I made pico-de-gallo so no need for tomatoes in the guac."

"Uh, oh. Second flaw. Guac must have some tomatoes."

"No, it doesn't. Just avocado and garlic salt is enough."

He picked up a knife, chopping tomatoes. "Actually, it should have more than just tomatoes, but I figure that's enough for now. "

Christie raised her hands. "See, that's how things start. Trivial things that don't matter take on greater meaning and cause problems."

Bryson moved over and grasped Christie's arms, bringing her to stand eye to eye with him. "You don't have to worry about me, Christie. I'm here for the long run—flaws and all."

Tears glistened in her eyes. "I'm...afraid." She couldn't believe she'd said the words aloud.

"I know. I am too. But I know that we're meant to be together. You're my kindred spirit. I feel it and I know you feel it too. Will our life be perfect? No. Far from it. But as long as we have love and we forgive each other our human frailties, we'll survive. No, let me change that. We'll thrive. I love you. I want to spend my life with you for however long or short it is. Please say yes."

She wanted to say she'd think it over, that she needed more time, the list of things went through her head. Instead, what came out was a quiet, "Yes."

He whooped and picked her up, twirling her around the room before setting her down and planting a full kiss on her lips.

"As soon as possible."

"Before some Armadillo Pie?"

"Some what? I hope that tastes better than it sounds."

She nodded. "It will, and I think I better finish them if you're wanting any pie this evening."

He gazed down at her. "You've made me so happy."

"I have?"

"Yes. I love pie."

Christie burst out laughing. She knew that being able to laugh together would make all the difference as they moved forward as a couple. She closed her eyes as she kissed him again, wondering how a forty year old woman could feel as giddy as a teenager.

CHAPTER NINE

The following day Christie texted Abby to see if she could stop by and deliver the pie. After getting the go-ahead, Christie drove out to the winery. Normally a hub of activity, the parking lot was empty, and silence cloaked the area. Heat rose from the gravel as she exited the truck, taking the pie keeper with her.

Abby had said she'd be at the winery so to stop by there instead of coming up to the house. Christie made her way to the door before calling out, "Hello! Abby, it's Christie."

Abby's voice echoed in the space. "I'm back here. Be there in a sec."

Christie walked over to one of the vats. Toward the back was a set of metal stairs climbing up to a small ramp. A few newer looking vats didn't have ramps by them. She wondered what the difference was and why some had ramps on them. Which one had been the one that Abby's husband had fallen into. She'd like to do a closer inspection, but spied Abby headed her way, her hand raised in a wave.

"Hi, I figured that you'd be receiving food but wanted to bring this pie for you and your staff." Christie handed the pie keeper to Abby, the strain on her face evident.

"Thanks. I could put on some coffee, and we could have a slice now if you have time."

"Sure." Christie followed Abby into the primary office, moving through the first room and back into a break room area. As Abby scooped coffee into the coffeemaker's basket, Christie unfastened the plastic top to the pie keeper.

"Yum. That looks delicious." Abby said.

"It's pretty decadent. A shortbread type crust with a layer of sweetened cream cheese, then pudding, followed by fresh whipped cream with chocolate shavings."

"Sounds perfect. Hopefully, it'll put me in a sugar coma, so I don't have to think anymore." Abby stopped what she was doing. "Sorry, I shouldn't have said that."

"Don't mind me. I used to be a hospice nurse. I'm used to hearing all kinds of things. It's like we need a bit of macabre humor to deal with what's happened."

"Wow. I didn't know that you were a hospice nurse. I can't imagine doing that. I bet it would be such a sad and hard job."

"It can be, but it's also fulfilling, as you're able to help the person and the family as they're going through such a difficult period. They don't have to think about whom to call or what to do and you're able to provide a bit of peace during a chaotic time."

"Sounds a bit like an unsung hero."

"I don't know if I'd go that far." Christie replied.

"That's humility talking. I think that those who aren't recognized are often some of the greatest heroes we have in our midst."

Christie blushed at the praise. "I was just doing my job."

"I doubt it. Even though we don't know each other well, I feel like you have a very tender heart.

In some ways, it reminds me of Dax." She turned away from Christie as she wiped away tears with the back of her hand.

That was a surprise. Christie would have liked to press further on that statement, but Abby motioned with her hand, "Plates and silverware are over there. Should be something you can use to cut and serve the pie."

Christie retrieved the items, cutting two small pieces of pie. She set one on the table across from Abby as she took a seat. "I also came out because I wanted to make sure that you still wanted us to have that check for the rescue. If it's an issue, I wouldn't want to cause you any problems with your changed circumstances."

Abby sat down across from Christie. "I appreciate your asking, but I still want those funds to go to the rescue. In fact, I asked people if they wanted to honor Dax to give to the veteran's program at the rescue."

Christie replied, "That's terrific. Thanks."

Abby took a bite of the pie. "Oh, wow. That's yummy." The coffeepot beeped, signaling the brew was ready. Abby made to get up, but Christie stopped her.

"Let me."

"Thanks." Abby took another bite of the pie.

Christie poured two coffees and set them on the table, along with some creamer.

They ate in companionable silence until Abby finished her plate. "I may have to sneak another piece of that pie. It's so good."

"Here." Christie placed another sliver on her plate. "I want to express my condolences at your loss. I've never been married, so I can't imagine the pain though I've seen it etched on many spouses faces over the years."

Abby set her fork down and covered her face with her hands. Her body shook as sobs escaped her lips. "I'm sorry. My emotions are all over the place right now. What's that saying about being unlucky in love? I think my picture should be shown next to that statement."

"No need for apologies. Lots of times when someone dies, it can also bring up other times of grief." Christie couldn't believe she'd stoop so low as to try and get Abby to open up about her first husband's death. But she stopped short of asking about him.

Abby wiped her nose and stared into Christie's eyes. "Can I tell you something?"

Christie took a breath. What was Abby going to say? "Certainly."

"I'm…I can't believe I'm saying this. But I'm also, somewhat relieved." Tears streamed down her face. "I'm such a terrible person." Her face grew red as she tried to hold back more tears.

"That can be a common reaction, just like the emotions of anger, questioning and others. Especially if there were any issues involved that could contribute to it."

Abby nodded but didn't respond. Instead, she took a sip of the hot coffee, taking time to compose herself. "He's always had some issues from the war. He told me upfront and he'd been cognizant of them, working on it to get better. But the last few years, his moods were all over the place. It felt like walking on eggshells. You just never knew what was going to set him off."

"I'm sorry to hear that. I heard he had diabetes?"

"Yes. That didn't help either. He'd gotten better but with the heavy workload, he'd forget to eat or have something that caused problems with his blood sugar. And then all—well you know—broke loose. Later, he'd apologize but I could see it was getting to him too. He was frustrated and felt he was letting me down."

"Many men have the need to prove themselves. I'm sure that he knew you understood."

Abby wiped her face with a napkin. "It's fine. No point in thinking about it now. I've got to figure out what to do on top of everything else. This was his dream. Not mine. It may be a good time to take Ronald Lewis up on his offer."

This was news. If Ronald had made an offer to buy the winery this soon after Dax's death, that was callous. "Did he contact you since the funeral?"

"Oh no. He wanted to buy the property when it first came up for sale. We just outbid him."

"So, with Dax out of the way, this is an opportunity for him. Abby, I hate to be blunt, but have you considered that Dax's death wasn't an accident?"

"What are you implying? That Ronald killed Dax to get this place?" She shook her head. "No, I can't believe he'd stoop that far. He could have simply upped his bid. Plus, how would he know that Dax was by himself that day?"

Christie nodded. It made sense, plus how would he have gotten him up the stairs and then over into the vat? Dax had been a tall, heavy-set man while Ronald was older, and it was doubtful he was that strong. But something seemed off.

Abby rose from her seat and went over to her purse, where she retrieved a box of dental floss. "I have this one tooth that always bothers me. I'll just pop into the bathroom. Be back in a jiff." Abby left the room and Christie swallowed another sip of coffee.

It would make sense if Abby's husband had been abusive that she'd be relieved he was out of the picture. Yet, the image she'd heard of him from others, and now Abby, didn't gel with that view. Yes, abuse can be emotional too, but it didn't seem that he'd been physically abusive unless Abby was holding that back from Christie.

She glanced up as Abby returned. "I hope I'm not being insensitive, but what do you think happened?"

"I've been trying to figure that out myself. As far as I can gather, he must have slipped and hit his head before falling into the vat."

A thought came to Christie. "I noticed a lady sitting next to you at the funeral. Is that a friend or relative?"

"Oh, you mean Susan. She's Peter's sister."

Christie replied, "Peter? I don't think I know him."

"Oh, you wouldn't. He's my first husband. We were only married for a short while before he was killed in a car accident. I lived with survivor's guilt for a long time after it happened."

Christie picked up her coffee cup and took a sip. "Why do you say that?"

"I was going somewhere, can't recall right

now, and borrowed his Mercedes as it was roomier, and I was picking up some other ladies and driving. A club luncheon, I think. Anyway, he took my Porsche and—well, I guess it was the luck of the draw. We loved taking drives in that car."

Abby lost herself in the past while Christie thought about what Abby had said. Her car was a two-seater, and the pair often took drives in it. That meant that the accident could have killed both of them, or just Abby. Would Susan have benefitted from her brother's death? She had so many questions and no way to get answers. Instead, she turned back to the current situation.

Christie spoke to Abby. "You know, now that I think about it, the day I came over here, there was another accident with one of your employees. Was that the same staircase?"

"Now that you mention it. Yes. I don't know exactly what happened as I'd been in the office, but Cal had fallen and hit his head. Got a rather good size bruise on his forehead." She gazed off to the side, and Christie felt the woman wasn't telling her the full truth of what had transpired.

"Wait, so it wasn't from falling down the stairs?"

Abby shook her head. "No. He tripped going up the stairs. Why are you asking?"

"I can't help it. I've always been curious about things like that."

"You know what they say about curiosity and the cat." Abby winked.

A chill ran up Christie's spine. Was that simply a statement made in jest or a threat? Abby seemed nice enough but was she putting on an act to keep Christie on her side? Maybe the young woman was really relieved because she thought she'd gotten away with murder.

She stood. "Well, I've kept you long enough. Again, I'm really sorry about what's happened. Please contact me if you need anything."

"Thanks for the pie. It was delicious and I'm not sure how much my staff will have. I may have to get your recipe."

"Be happy to send it to you."

They walked out of the office together and

Christie got into her truck. A feeling of dread came over her. Were the two accidents at the winery related or simply a coincidence?

CHAPTER TEN

Following the craziness of the last weeks, Christie was ready to focus on work at the nonprofit. After leaving Abby, she wanted to put the tragic events behind her. There were far too many questions that she couldn't find out the answers to and so it was best to let it go.

She also needed to get back on track to eating better. She'd sent the other pie home with Bryson, but two slices of pie wasn't a good start on healthy eating. She sighed at the raw veggies and hummus that she'd brought with her to work for her afternoon snack. She could do this. Christie picked up a carrot, dipping it into the hummus before crunching down on the carrot.

Now that she'd been given the go-ahead on cashing the check from Abby, she wanted to draft a budget for where she felt the money would be best allotted. Then she'd let Lana look it over before they presented it to the board.

She crunched on a piece of celery, one of the

strings getting stuck in her teeth. She should be like Abby and keep dental floss in her purse. That would make it easier in case any food got stuck. Much easier than using a toothpick or your fingers. Her mind wandered for a moment. Something was trying to come to the surface, but she couldn't grasp it. Sighing, she focused back on the spreadsheet, while the elusive thought kept knocking like a woodpecker. Then, out of the blue, it came to her.

How do you fall up steps?

You could place your foot wrong, thus missing the next step. You could hit your toes against the stair tread or lose your grip on the railing. For Abby's husband to hit his head, it had to be close to the top step. So, did he then stagger backwards into the vat?

Christie couldn't let it go. Something kept nagging at her about what happened. She grabbed her purse, deciding to make an unscheduled trip over to the winery. She could say that she'd been in the area and decided to check in on Abby and see how she's doing.

The drive over passed quickly and when she arrived, there weren't any cars in the parking lot. Had everything come to a standstill since Dax's death?

Christie walked over to the door, which was unlocked, though the inside interior only had a few lights on.

"Hello? Anyone here? Abby, It's Christie."

No answer came back.

Christie glanced over at the office, the blinds closed and a light behind it. She started towards it, but at the last minute moved toward the large vat where she believed the accident had occurred. A set of metal stairs led up to the top. She set her purse down by the bottom of the steps.

A noise made her turn around. "Hello? Abby, is that you?"

No answer.

Christie waited. It must have been some outside road noise. She climbed the steps, looking at the treads as she made her way up to the top. She grabbed the bar that encompassed the ramp at the top of the vat, steadying herself as the open stairway felt less secure up here. The container was closed and had been emptied. She lifted an edge, but all she could see was darkness. A fruity and yeasty smell enveloped her before she lowered the top back down.

Hairs rose on her arms as she shivered.

Someone was watching her.

She jerked back around to face the stairs. No one was there, but Christie could feel someone's presence in the building with her. Surely Abby would respond to her calls. Scanning the building, she squinted into the dark corners, but could see nothing.

Christie gripped the rail tightly as she made her way gingerly down the steps, focusing on each tread. When she reached the bottom, she let go of the breath she'd been holding. Her nerves must have been playing tricks on her.

Turning to pick up her purse, she felt a rush of air behind her, but couldn't turn quickly enough. She screamed as someone shoved her hard and she stumbled forward toward a large metal foundation pole . She barely had time to raise her left arm to deflect from hitting her head against the pole, but her action threw off her balance and she landed hard on the cement floor. Her face hit the cement and she skid a bit on her arms before coming to a stop. The impact caused her to have her breath knocked out, and it took a moment as she gasped for air. Stunned by the fall, she knew she had to stay focused in case of a second attack. Thankfully, she heard someone running away allowing her to breathe easier.

Christie gulped in a large breath, coughing as she made her way onto her side. She could feel a rug burn on her cheek.

Or should it be called a cement burn? She chuckled to herself before gathering her emotions before she broke down in tears. Christie raised her hand to the tender spot as she blinked her eyes away from tears and to focus them against the darkened interior. She faced the vat and moved up to her knees, taking a minute to compose herself before trying to stand up. She felt that whoever had pushed was gone, but her senses were still on high alert. Even the silence bore a sinister air to it. Whoever had pushed her must have left the building the way she'd entered. Peering toward the space under the vat, she could see where the floor had been swept but some areas had accumulated dirt and dust next to spots where the broom couldn't reach. Sitting on the floor, Christie took stock of how she felt. Other than the fall, she didn't think she'd broken anything. Her arm hurt where she'd stuck it out to hinder her from hitting the pole and tomorrow she'd have a decent size bruise there.

Then she moved closer to the vat to see something that had caught her attention. It was a small piece of string. Christie reached over and picked it up.

No, not string.

Dental floss.

~

After ensuring she was okay, she rose from her spot, taking a moment to wipe down her jeans, thankful they'd taken more of the assault than her knees. Her face burnt and she felt its sting as she moved her mouth or squinted. Carefully taking up her purse, she held it tightly in her hand in case she needed to use it as a weapon. The space back to the front was fraught with tension as she constantly swiveled to ensure she wouldn't be attacked unawares again. Christie made it back to her truck, locking the doors behind her as she turned on the truck.

She opened her hand staring down at the small almost translucent strand. Floss was small but yet, like fishing line, had strength. What plausible reason would there be for it being there? Certainly, no one would use it around the vats as they had to keep those areas clean for inspection. That's why even the small space under the vats were clean. At least those accessible.

The discovery of the dental floss put her mind racing.

Could dental floss be strung across a stair, causing someone to trip? It was so light and transparent, most people wouldn't even notice it being there. By the time they'd looked down, they'd already have fallen.

But if it had been used to trip Dax, it would

still have been there when he was found. That is, if someone hadn't taken it before others arrived. Christie emitted a groan.

Oh Abby.

Christie had been the perfect alibi. Abby would set up the floss on the stair, knowing her husband would be going up the stairs while she was gone. He wouldn't have any reason to look at any of the steps as he'd gone up and down them numerous times. Then all she had to do was get rid of the floss. She could have easily stuck it in her bag and since she carried floss, it wouldn't even be an issue if they looked. She could then produce some excuse for it not being in the container. Though she'd have to also have some scissors or a knife. In her hurry to cut the floss, that one piece fell, and she didn't know it.

Plus, she'd dropped her bag while at the rescue, showing that she had some in her purse. Had it been on purpose in case some was found on scene? Christie felt like she'd been so used. Had Abby been setting her up as a pawn all this time, giving her compliments, making her feel comfortable so that she would support her in case anything pointed to it not being an accident?

Christie put her head in her hands when a rap on her window startled her.

CHAPTER ELEVEN

Christie jolted upright to see an older man, face lined from the sun and hard work, standing there. She didn't recognize him from the last time she'd been at the winery.

His strong voice carried through the window. "Are you okay?"

She started to roll her window down and then thought better of it. "Yes, I'm fine. I just came to see if Abby was here." Thankfully, where she'd bruised her face was the opposite side from the window or it could bring on some questions she didn't feel confident answering.

He continued, "She's out for a few days, taking some time to think about the next steps for the winery. Can I give her a message?"

"If you'll let her know that I stopped by. Christie. Christie Taylor."

"From the equine rescue?"

Christie nodded. "Yes, you know of it?"

"Yes, it's been an immense help for my grandson. He does equine therapy there. Thanks for doing what you do. We were all so worried about him after he came back." He stopped, his jaw clenching at what must have been some tough emotion wanting to break through. "Anyway, thank you. It truly saved his life." He pressed his lips together before touching the brim of his cowboy hat. "I'll let Abby know you stopped by."

He made to walk away from the truck when a thought came to Christie. She let her window down. "Excuse me. There was a man that had an accident before the one with Abby's husband. Did they fix whatever had caused the problem?"

"I guess you could say that. Abby's husband shoved him, and he fell, causing him to cut his head." His expression turned, making Christie realize he hadn't meant to say that.

"They were in a fight?"

"Sorry, ma'am but I don't like talking ill about the dead. Now I best be off." He made to walk away from the truck.

"I certainly understand." She'd turned toward

him, forgetting the scrapes on her face.

He squinted at her, and she twisted her body so that she faced away and down, acting as if she were looking toward the key area. She glanced up as he nodded and walked toward the front of the building.

Whew. That was close. That's when Christie realized that there wasn't any other vehicle in the parking lot with her. So where had he come from? There must be another area where people working at the winery parked. If she'd known that, she might have been able to see who'd been there when she'd been attacked.

Learning that the two men had been fighting made Christie wonder what had caused the incident. However, it also meant that he hadn't been hurt in the same way that Dax may have sustained his injuries. Yet, if there'd been bad blood between the two men, why hadn't he been fired?

It didn't make sense that Dax would keep him on. Unless Dax was the one who'd started the fight and didn't want to have Cal create even more trouble. But for now, she needed to head home so she could take stock of her injuries. A nice Epsom salt bath may be in order so that she wouldn't be sore tomorrow.

She put the truck in reverse, backing out of the parking lot to head toward home. She had just made it to the main road when the tears started flowing. She'd been lucky that whoever had been in the large room with her had only pushed her. She pushed in the phone to make a call.

A man's voice answered.

"Bryson. Can you come over to my house later?"

"Christie, honey, what's wrong?"

The events spilled out as she choked back the sobs.

"I'm coming right now."

"No. I'm fine. Plus, I want to soak in a hot bath."

"I don't want you by yourself. Are you sure you're not hurt worse?"

"Yes. I'm just shook up. Please don't worry. You can come over later."

"Okay. "

Christie made it to the house, only to find Bryson waiting for her. Instead of being upset that he had come early, she was relieved.

He was striding toward her as she exited the truck, collapsing into his arms as tears streamed down her face.

"I'm here."

Two simple words, but oh how they meant everything. How had she not realized the need to know that someone would be there to gather her up in the safety of their arms?

She pulled back to wipe at her eyes when she saw Bryson's shocked expression.

"What is it?"

"Have you not seen the side of your face?"

"No. I just wanted to get home."

"Lean on me. Are you hurt anywhere else? Should we go into town to the urgent clinic, and have you checked out?"

Christie shook her head. "No, more that my pride was hurt. I wasn't paying attention, and that's why someone could shove me. I knew I'd hit the ground and must have caused the harm on my face when I slid a bit when I landed. I was more concerned that I'd possibly fractured my arm trying to stop the fall."

Bryson escorted her as she gingerly made her way up the stairs. When they were inside the house, he put her into a chair. "You sit here. I'll run your bath for you. Where's the Epsom salt?"

"Under the counter in the bathroom cabinet." She leaned against the soft back of the chair as the adrenaline left her body. In a few moments, Bryson returned.

"The bath should be ready soon. Are you sure you'll be all right on your own, or do I need to wait here until you're finished?"

"I'm okay. I guess I'm a bit shook-up about it."

"And no wonder. You're going to have a nice shiner on your right side, plus some scraping there. Any arnica gel on hand?"

"No. I can get some—"

"Absolutely not. I'll run into Boerne and pick some up at Nature's Presence. Should I stop by and let Pop know on my way back?"

"I'll call him. Probably best if he thinks I just took a fall. You know how he worries." She shared a smile with Bryson.

"Okay. But I want you to lock this door behind me. I won't be gone long, but I'm not crazy about you being here by yourself."

Christie shivered. Would whoever had pushed her come after her at her home?

"I'll do that."

"Okay, back soon. Love you." He placed a kiss on her forehead.

"Love you too. Thank you."

Christie locked the door behind him and made her way into the bedroom, where she stripped off her clothing. She gasped when she glimpsed her face in the mirror. She felt the tender, red areas where her face had slid on the ground. The arnica would help a lot with its healing. As she climbed into the tub of hot water, she felt the tension release from her shoulders. Laying her head back against the rim, she allowed the tears to fall onto her cheeks. What had Abby said about curiosity killing the cat?

She may not have been killed, but she could have been seriously hurt. Her arm didn't seem to have any issues, though she'd keep an eye on it tonight.

Christie wanted to remember about what she's seen at the winery, but her mind was having none of it. As the water grew cold, she dried herself off and pulled on a pair of leggings and a warm sweatshirt before climbing onto her bed, immediately falling into a dreamless sleep.

The sound of rapping woke her. She blinked as she worked to get her mind around where she was as the bedroom had grown dark while she slept. Turning over, she noted that the blanket from the bench at the end of her bed covered her. She didn't remember grabbing it. Looking at the clock, she saw it was six thirty. She'd been asleep for a while. No wonder she felt groggy. In a way, she should be thankful that she hadn't hit her head as she would have received a concussion. A scraped face would as least be an easier time of healing.

Christie sat up in bed before pushing the

blanket off her. She let out a groan as her body protested with a dull pain from its earlier fall. She made her way to the front door, where Bryson stood outside. He waved, and she opened the door.

"HI ya. How ya feeling?"

"A bit like a truck ran over me. Have you been here long?"

"Nope. Pop wanted me to come get you. He's got dinner on and it's about ready."

Christie ran her fingers through her tangled hair. "I don't know..." Her stomach rumbled. "Okay, my body says yes even if my mind says no. I'll be a few minutes."

"All good. I'll wait." He took a seat in a nearby chair as Christie went into her bathroom. Her face had already begun its changing of colors to a sickly yellow-greenish tone, along with a nasty purple. She looked on the counter. There sat a tube of arnica gel. Had Bryson been here while she was sleeping? If so, how'd he get inside?

She walked back out to the living room, holding the tube in her hand.

"Oh good. Glad you found it. I figured you'd want it when you woke up."

"How'd you get in?"

Bryson motioned with his head. "Pop waved me down, and I let him know what was going on. I told him I was going into town for the ointment, and he gave me his key in case you were still sleeping. You were sleeping so deeply, I didn't want to wake you. Though I almost did in case you had a concussion. But I figured you'd already know if you did, so I left the ointment and went back over to chat with him for a while. I'm rambling, aren't I?" He grinned.

She smiled at him, placing her hand on his cheek for a minute. "Yes, but it's okay. Did you put the blanket over me?"

"Yep. I thought you might get cold and this way you wouldn't wake up. Hope that was okay."

Christie nodded. "Thanks. I'm just surprised that I didn't wake up when you came in."

"I already told you. Your subconscious knows I'm a good guy." He winked. "Do you need me to put some of that on your face for you?"

"No, I can manage. Thanks. So, Pop made dinner?"

"Yep. And let me tell you, it smells wonderful. Pot roast, carrots, potatoes, along with brown gravy and biscuits. My contribution was some broccoli with cheese sauce I grabbed at HEB."

"That sounds good. I won't be too long." Christie went back into the bathroom, where she brushed her teeth and gingerly washed her face before applying the gel. Her hair brushed, she pulled it up into a high ponytail. Deciding not to change, she slipped her feet into some slides before heading out to where Bryson waited for her. They walked down the stairs and Bryson helped her up into the truck, a groan escaping her lips as she felt the tenderness on her knees.

"Oh, should we take the rest of the pie over to Pop's?"

"Good idea. Back in a jiff." Bryson moved out of the truck and up the stairs in a flash, coming down holding the remains of the creamy creation, which he handed to Christie.

"Now, let's go get some grub."

"Sounds like what Pop would say. I think you're spending too much time around him."

Bryson started the truck. "I like spending time with him. He's a great guy. Some of his stories are hilarious."

Christie smiled. "Well better you than me. I've already heard them so many times I can recite them from heart."

"Which is good as they'll always be a treasured memory of him."

A lump gathered in Christie's throat. She knew that Pop couldn't live forever, but she hated the idea of him being gone. For now, she'd make sure that she spent as much time with him as she could.

CHAPTER TWELVE

Pop was pulling the plates from the dish cabinet when they entered. He set them down before enveloping Christie in a big hug. "Come here, girly. If I get my hands on whoever done this, there's gonna be you-know-what to pay."

"Thanks, Pop."

"What were you thinking going over to where someone died recently—even if it was an accident?"

Christie lowered herself into the oak chair Bryson had pulled out for her. "That's the thing. I don't think it was an accident."

"Okay, hold that thought. For now, let's get these vittles on the table and get some warm nourishment in you."

"Pop, what can I do to help?"

"Nothing. Let us handle it." Pop waved toward a plate of biscuits that Bryson set on the table, along with a stick of butter.

"I'm good with that." Christie smiled.

"Liar." Bryson laughed.

Christie joined in. "Okay, you know me. I hate not doing something."

"We know!" The two men chimed in unison.

Christie put her arms across her chest. "I'm not that bad."

Bryson and Pop made eye contact before bursting out laughing.

"You guys. Two peas in a pod." Christie set the plates Bryson handed her in front of three seats. After all the items had been placed on the table, Pop said a prayer and they piled their plates with the meat, vegetables, and rich brown gravy. Christie popped a piece of biscuit into the pan gravy before signaling her pleasure with a "Ummm. So good."

Bryson asked, "So, spill. What makes you think the death wasn't an accident?"

Christie swallowed before dabbing at her lips with a napkin. "Too many things don't make sense. Plus, today when I fell, I could see under the vat. It's up on steel legs and while it'd been swept, I noticed something up next to one leg.

"What was it?" Bryson speared some broccoli.

"Dental floss."

"Whadya say?" Pop responded.

"I saw a small piece of dental floss. I put it in my jeans."

"How in tarnation does a piece of dental floss have anything to do with all this?"

"That's what I wondered. But here's what I know. Abby's purse fell open while she was at the rescue. One thing that dropped out was dental floss. She grabbed at it first. Wouldn't you have reached for your wallet or phone first?"

Bryson answered. "Not necessarily. It could have been that it was closer to her. But for the benefit of the doubt, are you saying that she didn't want you to see it?"

"That's what I'm thinking. I've been trying to wrap my brain around how someone could trip and fall into the vat of wine and not try at least to get out. That means he either hit his head hard enough that it knocked him unconscious, or there was already an issue with his blood sugar."

"Oh yeah, I remember something about him

having diabetes." Bryson said.

"But the main thing would be that he has to hit his head. So how to control that and make it look like an accident? The dental floss must have been wrapped on the top stair tread where he wouldn't look. He'd already be looking toward the vat. Especially if someone had left it open, and he wanted to close it."

"Continue." Bryson popped a roasted carrot into his mouth.

"Let's say that Abby knows that the first suspect is always the spouse. She sets up the floss, which is pretty much clear in color, on the stairs. Then she heads over to the rescue, thus giving her an alibi. Her husband climbs the stairs and trips, causing him to hit his head on the metal bar."

"But that doesn't take into account how he got into the vat or drowning." Bryson responded.

"Well, he could have staggered backwards and fallen in. Again, we don't know if his sugar was low or what was going on at that moment. At this point, it's mainly conjecture."

Bryson responded. "Okay, so let's say that's

how this went down. The deputies would see the floss when they got there."

"Not if Abby ran in, cut the floss, and then called the sheriff's office. Wait a minute. She didn't call them. She called me. So that gave her even more time. She could have stuffed it in her purse or jacket and even if someone would have checked there, not sure it would have been seen. However, when it was cut, a piece that had been tied must have fallen in that small space close to the vat's leg."

Pop smeared some butter on his biscuit. "Have you spoken to the sheriff about it?"

"No. It's just something on my mind. I don't have any proof that's what actually occurred."

Pop set the biscuit down before ladling some more gravy on his plate over the potatoes. "Okay, it makes sense what you're saying. But what's the motive?"

"I'm not sure, but Abby had bruises on her arms. She said they were from working in the winery, but what if she were actually showing them to me so I'd think it was her husband who had done it?"

Pop shook his head. "We've been over this before. No way he was that type of man. And I've known some real jerks in my day. Terrible to their wife and kids, but sweet as pie when they'd show up at church. Nope, I'd bet my reputation on it."

"Then what do you think, Pop?"

"Don't rightly know, but not much you or I can do about it. Best leave it to the professionals. And no more going over there by yourself. If there is a killer out there, then you're mighty lucky that the only thing that happened is you got banged up a bit. You don't want them thinking you know what happened and come after you next. This old ticker can't handle you getting hurt, darlin."

Bryson nodded. "I agree with Pop. You could have been seriously injured or worse. Do you think it was Abby who shoved you?"

"I couldn't tell. It certainly could have been a man or a woman. Because it was so quick, it caught me off guard and when I stumbled, I couldn't catch myself before I fell. I only had time to raise my arm to deflect it from my head hitting, but that's what caused me to fall and slide, so not sure if it helped me or caused it to be worse."

Bryson dipped a piece of meat in the gravy. "Those situations you just act on instinct, you don't think. Your brain just commands the body to do something. I've had some situations with work where I've seen guys who couldn't tell you what or why they reacted the way they did."

Pop nodded agreement before turning back to Christie. "But you hadn't seen Abby or anyone else when you got there?"

Christie shook her head. "No. In fact, it was really quiet. It was only when I left that one of their staff came up to my truck."

"Wait, could that have been the person who shoved you?"

"I, well, I don't know. But I don't think so. He'd just arrived. At least, that's how it appeared. Plus, what would be his reasoning for doing it?"

She stretched in her seat, grimacing a bit as her muscles complained. "I do think something happened there. Whether Abby did it or not, someone was not wanting me looking around."

Christie faced Bryson. "I want to go back over there. Will you go with me?"

"What do you expect to learn?"

"I don't know, but I feel like maybe I was shoved because there was something else someone didn't want me to see."

"All right. We can go tomorrow." He squeezed her hand in his.

"Thanks." Christie replied.

"Well, now that you got that settled, who's ready for pie?" Pop rose from the table.

Christie groaned. "I'm stuffed."

"So does that mean you don't want pie?"

"Absolutely not."

CHAPTER THIRTEEN

Christie took a few days sick leave to recover. It would be easier to go back to the office without all the questions on what happened to her face or to bring any more attention to it.

Bryson texted in the morning to see how she was feeling, and she spent the time reorganizing closets and doing some cleaning she'd been neglecting. Around lunchtime, the phone rang. It was Bryson.

"Hi, just checking up on you. Feeling better?"

"Yes, I think I needed a few days to work out the kinks, but the bruising and scrapes on my face are already much better, too."

"Good. Hey, just wanted to let you know that I heard that Roland Lewis is all upset as he'd been talking to Abby about buying the property after Dax died. But he hasn't been able to get ahold of her. Have you been in touch with her since the funeral?"

"No. Not since our last conversation. I never

saw her the day someone pushed me and the more I've thought about it, I don't think it was her. Just doesn't make any sense. Why would she push me? There could have been an off-chance I would have seen her or recognized her, and she'd want me on her side if I'm her alibi. No, I think it was someone else that shoved me."

"Who do you think it was?"

Christie lowered herself onto the bed while continuing, "I'm not sure. But it makes me wonder if I came in when they were looking for something."

"I thought you said no one was there when you arrived?"

"That's what I thought, but then I realized that there was parking that's hidden from the front. Probably put it in so that they'd have parking for staff in the back and parking for customers in the front lot. Someone could have parked back there so as not to be seen there."

"Hmm, then that would indicate someone that worked there."

"Possibly. That or they drove around and

found the parking area that was hidden from the front."

"Makes sense. Well, I need to get back to work. I'll call you later. And if there's anything you need, give me a holler."

"Will do. Thanks for calling." Christie ended the call and leaned back against the headboard.

Where was Abby?

She texted the woman, but there was no response. She should drive back out to the winery and see if more people were there. There had to be a reason she wasn't replying to Christie's texts. Either she was busy, or she was ignoring her for a reason, though Christie wouldn't know why. Unless Christie's questions had made Abby leerier of saying the wrong thing. She had admitted to Christie that Dax's death had been something of a relief. If Christie was called on to speak to the sheriff, that wouldn't be a good thing to say in her defense.

Then, of course, there was the matter of insurance where Dax was concerned. She needed to find out about that. Maybe Abby's money was running low, or she decided that she could add to it by getting rid of Dax. She wouldn't be the first wife to kill her husband for the insurance money—even the rich ones.

With the winery moving forward at a quick pace, she may have needed to replenish her funds. But then why would she give such a large donation to the rescue? To gain Christie's help or even, if necessary, her silence?

She rose from the bed and went back to organizing, groaning as she twisted to place a box on an upper shelf. That fall was taking some time to get over. After deciding another Epsom salt bath would be a good idea, Christie dressed before heading over to Pop's house. His truck was gone, so he must be visiting with Curtis. She made her way over to the winery, already hearing the admonition from Pop and Bryson about not returning there. Hopefully, she could go without having to tell them about it. Plus, she wouldn't go in if there weren't lots of people around. And she could plead forgiveness versus permission if they called her on it. Thankfully, when she arrived the place was a hub of activity. That's probably why Abby hadn't responded to her call. She would be doing the work of two people now along with dealing with her grief. She went home and into bed as soon as she got done at the winery for the day. It made sense that she'd push returning any phone calls to later and Christie felt it made perfect sense.

Christie slid off her truck seat as she held the door open. She spied the man who'd knocked on her truck window a few days earlier.

"Hello, excuse me."

"Can I help ya, ma'am?" He shielded his eyes with his hand.

Christie drew closer. "We met the other day. You came over to my truck."

"Oh, sure. What can I do you for?"

"I'm looking for Abby. Is she around?"

He shook his head. "No. We all got notice to finish up the batch that's in the vats, but it's the last we've heard from her."

"She called you?"

He shook his head. "No, ma'am. Texted Mick,

the supervisor. I guess Ms. Abby's gonna go head and sell to Roland Lewis."

"You seem surprised by that."

"Truth be told, I am a bit. Last I heard from her, she wanted to think about it but was leaning toward keeping it going. From what some said, she didn't like the idea of picking up sticks and moving so soon again."

"Hmm. I tried calling and texting her but I'm not getting any answer. Any way I can get her address? I'd really like to go out and check up on her."

He wiped a red bandanna across his neck before stuffing the twisted cloth into his back pocket. "Not sure I can do that. If you'll follow me, you can ask the foreman if he'll give it to ya."

"I'd appreciate it." Christie followed behind him and the young man whistled across the din of the noise in the barn. "Cal. This lady' d like to speak with ya."

The man said something to two others and then moved to join them.

"Ma'am. I'll leave ya to it." He moved to join

the rest of the crew.

A burly man reached out with a calloused hand. "Howdy. What can I help you with?"

So, this was Cal. She noticed the scrape on his forehead, now healing and no longer covered by a bandage. He and Dax were about the same build so if they'd fought, it would've been an equal fight physically. If Cal was the supervisor, is that why Dax hadn't fired him? Maybe he wanted to ensure the timing over getting rid of an employee.

"I'm Christie Taylor. I work over at the horse rescue. I'd been speaking with Abby, and she isn't answering my calls or texts. I know this is a hard time, but I thought I'd check in on her."

His eyes flicked to the side of Christie's face, and she unconsciously raised her hand toward it. "Bad fall."

He didn't reply to her statement. Instead, he moved toward the office. "Follow me."

Christie went inside and he closed the door behind her. She moved away from him as his eyes narrowed, focused on her. "What do you want with Abby?"

"I was wondering if I might get her home address. I think with everything that's happened and her not knowing many people here, she may feel all alone after Dax's death. I'd like to let her know that I'm here for her if she needs anything."

He leaned back against the desk, crossing his arms in front of his massive bulk. Christie knew he was taking stock of her and if she was the sort of person who should be given any of that information.

Finally, he sighed and stood up from the desk. "I guess it won't hurt for you to have it. I've been worried about Abby, too."

"You have? Why?"

"She hasn't been herself lately. I don't think she'd do anything, but—"

"You mean, you think she would do something foolish?"

He shrugged. "People do crazy things. You never know what they're really thinking. I'm sure she's just taking some time for herself." He wrote the address on a piece of scrap paper he retrieved from the recycle bin.

"Thanks, I appreciate it."

"You're welcome. Now best get back to the work."

Christie followed him back out to the large, accessible area. "Did Abby give you all any indication of what she planned to do after you finished this?"

He shook his head. "Nope."

"And you spoke with her?"

"She texted me."

"When was that?" Christie asked.

"Few days ago. Why do you want to know?"

"Just curious. Thanks again for the address." She held up the paper.

"You're welcome. If you see Abby, tell her that I got her back."

That sounded strange but Christie nodded.

Plugging in the GPS she headed toward Herman Sons road. After spending some time driving, she spied the turnoff for the house. Luckily, the gate was open, and Christie drove through it. The house was a modern new build with the traditional look of south Texas limestone walls and a sheet-metal roof. She pulled up to the house and texted Abby again to let her know she was outside.

No response.

Climbing out of the truck's cab, she made her way to the front entrance and rang the doorbell, but no one came to the entry. Christie waited for a minute and then rang the bell again. Still no answer.

Perhaps Abby had gone into town.

She walked over to the carport on the side of the house but was surprised to see both vehicles parked there. Possibly she was in the back. Christie walked around the side of the home, calling out as she went. The backyard had been beautifully landscaped with a pool and an outdoor entertainment area.

Christie took in the firepit adjoining the pool and patio. "Nice." She made her way along the walk until she pulled open a short gate that led to a patio door at the back. The door's window coverings were open, and a large fluffy calico cat came running up to the door, meowing.

Christie bent down. "Hello you. Now I know where they got the name for the winery. Doesn't look like you've ever missed a meal." The cat meowed in response, twirling around Christie's legs. She bent down and picked up the cat who settled in her arms as she continued, "Where's your mama?"

The cat's meows continued.

Something didn't feel right.

Christie tried the door to find it unlocked. "Abby!"

The house was silent except for the sounds from the cat who she set down on the floor.

Christie spoke to the cat. "Hey you. Where's everyone?"

She made her way toward the huge gourmet kitchen, calling Abby's name as she went. In the kitchen, she noticed the cat bowl empty and the water almost gone from the dispenser. She refilled the water and found a tin of cat food. She placed it down on the floor, and the cat set to purring as he devoured the food. Christie spied a dry food timed container, so she filled it up and left it set to open later that day.

Once she'd completed these tasks, she moved toward the front of the house. Everything was neat and tidy. She then made her way down the hall to the bedroom. Here it looked like a tornado had come through. Christie stepped back from the door. Either Abby had gone crazy and had thrown things around the room, destroying vases, and pulling down shades or there had been a fight here. The hairs on the back of her neck bristled as she spied another patio door open, curtains flapping in the breeze.

"Abby! Can you hear me?" She yelled into the silence.

Nothing.

Christie returned the way she'd come in and as she made her way toward the back of the house, she spied Abby's purse and keys sitting on a side counter.

She wouldn't have left without those.

The cat jumped up next to the purse, causing it to fall to the floor. Christie jumped as the purse items and keys crashed to the ground.

Christie dialed the emergency line on her phone.

As the operator answered, she blurted out, "Hello. This is Christie Taylor. I think I may have stumbled on a..."

She thought fast. Cars in the drive, purse still here. What looked like a struggle.

"I think Abby Calhan is missing."

CHAPTER FOURTEEN

As Christie waited for the deputies to show up, she looked around. She knew better than to touch anything, but she grabbed her phone and snapped photos of the purse on the floor, along with Abby's keys, before heading to the bedroom. The sheets were pulled from off the bed and drawers open like someone had been going through them quickly, looking for something.

What was it?

As she took photos of the room, it felt off somehow. She went over to the bed and felt it. Cold.

On impulse, she rushed over to the guest wing. The beds were made, and it didn't look like she'd used these rooms. Poking her head into the adjoining bath, Christie noted that it looked like it had been used and then straightened. Perhaps Abby had stayed in one of the guest rooms instead of the master bedroom. It could explain the mess.

Who hasn't wanted to lash out in anger or grief at some point in their life? She'd done that in the master bedroom and hadn't cleaned it up yet. Though the disarray in the master bedroom didn't explain where she was now. And wouldn't she have done something in the closet? It didn't look to have anything out of place. Either Abby had been upset and started throwing things around or it was someone else entirely who had done it.

Wait. Christie rushed back into the kitchen, yelling for Abby along the way. No answer.

Forgetting herself and knowing better than to touch anything, Christie grabbed Abby's key ring before rushing out to the vehicles parked under the large, covered carport. If Abby was in one of the vehicles, she needed to find out in case Abby was injured and needed help. Gulping down her fear, she hit the key fob, unlocking the trunk. Christie took in a deep breath before moving closer to inspect the trunk's interior. Thankfully, it was empty. The interior of the truck parked next to the SUV also yielded no results.

Christie let out a sigh of relief, thankful that

Abby hadn't been found hurt—or worse—in one of them. She scanned the area. The quiet was prevalent, helping her to take a moment to calm her breathing, which was short and shallow. Knowing that she needed to stop for a minute and collect her thoughts, Christie took in five deep breaths. In. Out. In. Out. She felt the adrenaline calming and the oxygen providing her with more clarity.

Deciding she'd rather stay outside than in the house, Christie returned to the pool area in the back of the house. The pool would be inviting on a sweltering summer day with its cool blue walls and easy stairs into its depths.

Christie sat down in a canvas lounge chair next to a small glass table. She scanned the area beyond the main yard and pool area. Scrub oak and mesquite trees along the back section formed a break from the expanse of rocky caliche that traversed the expanse of the property. In the far corner, a large barn-type utility shed was partially hidden behind some fencing and tall bushes. She stood to go check it out when the sounds of tires on gravel met her ears.

Walking back to the front of the house, she was surprised to find a woman getting out of a white Land Rover that looked like Abby's. She shielded her eyes with her hands.

It was the woman sitting next to Abby at the funeral. She sought through her memory for the woman's name. Susan.

The woman waved. "Hello there!"

"Hello, I'm sorry. I don't think we've met, though I remember seeing you at Dax's funeral."

"I'm Susan. Yes, Abby pointed you out that day, but we weren't able to speak. There were so many people wanting to share their condolences, and I didn't want to leave Abby's side to come over and introduce myself."

"Understandable." Though she hadn't been next to Abby when they'd gone over to talk to her. Possibly it had been earlier that Susan had been referring to with Abby. Christie felt a nudge like she'd seen this woman before, but where?

Susan made to walk to the house. "Are you here to visit Abby too?"

Christie nodded. "I wanted to stop by and see how she's doing, but afraid she's not here."

"Oh, really. Not to worry, I have a set of keys."

"You do?" Christie asked.

"Yes, Abby said there was no point in me staying at a hotel when she had plenty of space here."

"Oh. Do you know where she is?"

A slight hesitation before she answered, "She's not inside?"

"No. And her purse and keys are still here."

Susan's gaze fixed on Christie. "You've been inside?"

Christie felt a stab of guilt rise in her throat. "I was worried about her, so I went around the back and the door was standing open. When I went inside is when I found her purse and keys." She held out the keys.

"Maybe she went for a walk." Susan waved her hand toward the property. "Or probably made a run to the store or over to the winery."

"Um, possibly." While people could walk their property, chances are Abby wasn't that type of person. As for heading to the store or the winery, unless they had a third vehicle Christie didn't know about, both vehicles were at the house. She started to say as much when she heard more tires on the gravel drive approaching.

They turned towards them as the deputies pulled up in their cruisers. It was the same deputy that Christie had spoken with the other day at the Fat Cat Winery.

"Hello again."

He pulled his glasses from his eyes before tucking them in his pocket. Christie watched as he rapidly went through his mind, trying to place her. "Oh, yes. Hello. Ma'am." He touched his head toward Susan as Christie noted his name plate showed Graves.

"Officer." Susan replied. "I mean, deputy."

"All good. Now you believe there's a missing person here?"

"What?" Susan exclaimed.

"I couldn't find Abby, and it looks like there may have been a struggle in the master bedroom."

Susan rushed toward the front door, but

Deputy Graves halted her. "Ma'am, I'd thank you for waiting out here until we go in and look around."

"But—"

"Stay here." He ordered, his voice firm and deep.

Christie watched as they pulled their guns from their holsters before Graves went to the front and the other deputy went around the back. His radio crackled as the pair of women watched him enter the house.

They waited, their talking ceased until they heard Graves call out, "Clear." The other deputy echoed it.

Christie let out a deep sigh. She spied Susan moving toward her vehicle. Her face toward the ground in contemplation, she jolted when Christie called out to her.

"You okay Susan?"

"What? Oh, yes. Fine." She moved back toward Christie as the deputies came outside.

Deputy Graves came up to the women. "You called this in?"

Christie nodded. "I came over to see if Abby was okay. She didn't answer the front door, but since I could see both cars were here, I figured she was inside."

"You didn't think that maybe she just wanted to be alone and chose not to answer the door to you?"

She bristled at his tone. "Well, no."

"Continue."

"I went around back and that's when I saw the cat and the door was unlocked, so I went inside."

"You didn't have permission to enter the premises by the owner?"

"I told you. I was concerned for her. That's all."

He stared at her without responding.

Christie continued, "Anyway, that's when I saw her purse and keys." She handed him the keys.

He frowned. "You moved these?"

"I thought she might be in the vehicle. I just wanted to make sure."

He sniffed. "You have a vivid imagination?"

Christie crossed her arms. "Is that a question or a statement?"

Ignoring her, he responded, "Are you a friend of Ms. Calhan?"

"Um, no. Well, yes."

"Which is it?"

Christie sighed. "It's a bit complicated. We're not friends in the regular or best buddies sense. Not really. But friendly acquaintances." She stopped, realizing she was babbling nonsense.

"But she called me when she found Dax."

"So let me get this straight. You're not friends and the first person she thinks to call on finding her husband dead is you?"

That sounded a bit strange, even to Christie. "Listen, I don't think that they know that many people here other than those that work for her. At least that's what I think." Christie looked to Susan for some help, but the woman remained silent.

"Anyway, she'd been over to the rescue and my number was most likely at the top of her recent contacts on her phone. With the shock, she probably saw my number, knew I was close and called me."

Susan finally interjected herself into the conversation as she came over to stand beside Christie. "Deputy, I'm thankful that she was worried enough about Abby to come over. Now, are we able to go inside? It's getting a bit windy out here and I, for one, am getting cold."

"Should be okay. We need to ask some further questions, anyway."

The trio walked inside while the other deputy climbed into his car, starting on paperwork, or calling in his report.

Inside the house, Susan moved into the kitchen where she put the kettle on to boil. "I don't know about you all, but I'd like a nice cup of tea."

Christie watched Susan move easily around the kitchen, knowing where everything was. It was apparent that she had been in the kitchen before as she pulled a canister of tea bags and cups from cabinets.

Did Susan know anything about Abby's disappearance?

If Abby died, she was most likely the

benefactor as there were no kids involved or other family, at least to Christie's limited knowledge. Was Susan to blame for Abby's disappearance? She certainly seemed nonplussed about Abby's disappearance. Yet, no money would be paid out if they couldn't find her to supply a death certificate. Sometimes for years. That could only mean that Abby was already dead or being held against her will. And that her body would turn up later.

Susan's car. She'd appeared nervous about it.

Christie shot up from her seat. "I'll be back in a minute."

She rushed outside to where Susan's car was parked. Glancing inside, the front seats were empty. She reached for the back door and opened it.

"What are you doing?"

Susan's voice had changed from its melodious sweet, older lady to threatening in tone.

"I'm, oh sorry. I got mixed up. Your car looks just like Abby's." She shut the door and faced Susan.

"Her car is in the carport. Which you already know. Lying doesn't look good on you." She hit her key fob, locking the doors behind Christie before crossing her arms. "What did you expect to find?"

"Nothing. I'm—" She better shut up while she was ahead. The last thing she needed was to get on the wrong side of a possible murderer.

Susan came up close to Christie and lowered her voice, "If you know what's good for you, you'll stay out of this." She then turned when the deputy came to the door, her voice lightening. "Now, come on. Let's get some tea in you." Susan strode back into the house as Christie followed behind. What had she done?

~

After getting statements from the pair, Christie had been allowed to leave. Getting in her truck, she thought back to the day.

Where was Abby?

Had she gone somewhere on her own? But how did she get away from the house without taking one of the vehicles?

Then there was Susan, with her hot and cold personality. Christie had definitely felt threatened by her to stay out of things. Certainly, Susan didn't want anyone to interfere in what was a significant inheritance, if that was the case.

Christie drove home, thinking about the situation. She'd only known Abby for a brief time, so maybe she had simply taken a few days to grieve and didn't want to speak with anyone—even her. Susan could have driven her to some place for the day or a couple of days at Abby's request. Since Susan didn't know Christie, maybe she felt Christie was sticking her nose in where it didn't belong. If she'd only been trying to cover for Abby if she'd had a bit of a melt-down after Dax's death. It would be understandable. Yet wouldn't she have said something right away when she saw the deputies? Explained that it was all a misunderstanding. She hadn't. In fact, she'd seemed lost in her own world for a bit of time.

Needless to say, Abby would still have taken her purse. But truth be told, even that could be explained away easily. She most likely just changed purses. And since Susan would be driving, she didn't need to take any car keys either. Christie tried to think if her wallet had been in her purse when it had fallen on the floor, but she struggled to place it in her mind. Thankfully, she could look at the photos she'd taken earlier.

She'd made it to her house when her phone beeped. Looking down, she saw an unknown number. Christie steeled herself before answering the call.

"Hello?"

"Christie. Hi. This is Susan. Listen, I want to apologize for my behavior earlier. I just want what's best for Abby and I wasn't very nice. I hope you'll forgive me."

"It's fine. Tensions run a bit high in a situation like that. Any news about Abby?"

"Sadly, no. I'm staying here at the house again tonight. You know, after the deputies left, I looked for Abby's suitcases. I couldn't find them, though they may be somewhere I haven't looked. Anyway, I'll let you know if I hear anything from her."

"Thanks. It's good you could come here when Dax died."

"Oh, I was here before that."

"You were?"

"Yes, I arrived a few days before. I'm attending a conference in San Antonio this coming week and I told Abby about it. She said I should come here and enjoy the Hill Country for a while."

"Oh, so you'll skip the conference now?"

"Why would I do that?"

Christie wanted to say—because Abby is missing—but replied, "I just, I thought you might."

"No. I'm sure Abby will turn up soon."

Christie leaned back against the seat. "You sound very confident about that."

"I do?"

There was a moment of silence.

"Hello?" Christie asked.

"Sorry. I think it's always best to remain confident in these situations. Better to take the offensive versus defensive approach. I'm sure Abby appreciates all you've done for her and no need to do anything further. We believe it will all work out for the best. Must run now. Goodbye."

Christie stared at the phone. Had she just received an apology or a threat to back off? But more importantly, it was the simple word that Susan had used that stuck in her mind. We. If someone was working with Susan, that opened up a totally new can of worms.

Had Susan killed Dax and needed someone to help her escape?

CHAPTER FIFTEEN

Christie needed time to stop thinking about everything going on with Abby or Susan. After getting off the phone, she'd texted Abby saying that she would be happy to help Abby should she want to chat or need anything. There was no response which Christie expected, but she felt that she'd done what she could at this point. She hoped Abby was simply taking some time away from everyone because she felt bad about not controlling her rage. If so, it would make sense she might feel embarrassed if she knew that Christie had seen the wreckage at her house.

Realizing she needed to grab some things from the store, she drove into Boerne to get some shopping done at HEB. Grabbing a shopping cart, she made her way into the produce area, trying to figure out what she should make for dinner and have on hand for lunches and suppers for the week. Thankfully, there were easy options of items already chopped or ready-made meals but instead of helping, it was a bit overwhelming with all the choices. She knew better than to come to the store when she didn't have a list or was feeling a bit hungry.

She was checking out a salad kit when she heard a familiar voice behind her. It was the man she'd spoken to at the winery the other day. Christie turned toward him and noted that he wasn't alone. It was the man she'd seen on the road the other day. Next to Mr. Lewis, Cal joined them. She turned back toward the packages of lettuces since they hadn't seen her.

One voice carried over to her. It was Roland Lewis. "I can't keep waiting on this. Where is she?"

"If I knew, I'd tell ya. Could be she hightailed it out of here and went back to where-ever it was she came from. All I know is we're going to finish the current work. There was nothing about anything further than that."

"Cal, I thought you had a handle on all this. You've let me down."

Cal lowered his voice. "Roland, I've got it

under control. I told you I'd take care of it, and I did."

Roland crumbled as the men strode past Christie, who stayed facing down toward the bags of lettuce.

"Excuse me. Can I grab one of those?"

"Oh, sorry." Christie responded. She glanced over, seeking the men but they must have moved toward the back of the store, as she couldn't see or hear them anymore.

What had Cal meant that he'd taken care of it?

She couldn't focus on getting any real shopping done. She spied a woman with her hands full. "Hi, do you need a basket?"

The woman nodded. "Bless you. I always say I'm only going to get a few things, and well, you see how that goes."

"Totally understand. Please take mine. I don't need it."

The harried young woman replied, "Thanks again. Come on, Levi."

A boy of around three scurried over and grabbed hold of his mother's leggings with a firm grip. His wide, saucer eyes stared at Christie, who smiled at the boy sporting a curly mop of brown hair. "Have a great day."

"You too." The woman hoisted the boy onto her hip in a familiar practiced motion as she went back to her shopping.

Leaving the produce aisle, Christie passed the wine aisle. There was a lot of money tied up in the Fat Cat Winery. The property was worth a lot of money, along with the production facilities. It could easily be split into the section where the winery stood and sell off the other property. No wonder Roland Lewis was so desperate to get his hands on it. It would enlarge his property and he could either keep, sell, or dismantle the facility. If Cal had been working for him all along, that could be why they were having so many setbacks at the winery. Though it would seem that doing that would delay things further. Unless the idea was to make it seem more trouble than it was worth, so Lewis could come in with a lower bid.

It could also explain why Cal and Dax had gotten into a fight. Christie wished she could ask

Abby about the confrontation, as it might give her some insights into what had caused the men to get into it with each other.

The entire incident this morning had drained her emotionally, and she just wanted to check out and get home. Nothing appealed, so she made her way up and down aisles, picking items up only to return them a few minutes later. A ride on Champ would clear her head. Walking to the freezers, she grabbed a couple of dinners she could stick in the microwave. She paid for the groceries and made her way out to her truck. Standing next to her driver's side door was Cal.

"Um, hello."

"Where's Abby?"

Christie stepped back. "Why are you asking me? I don't know."

"She spoke about you and the rescue a lot. I figured you were pals."

Christie tightened her grip on the grocery bag. "Well, you figured wrong. Even if I knew, I doubt I'd tell you."

He took a step toward her. "That wouldn't

be—"

A young woman's voice interrupted him. It was the lady that Christie had given her basket.

The little boy squirmed against her. "All good here?"

"Yes. I'm leaving right now." Christie made to open the truck's door, forcing Cal to back up toward the curb as he glared at her. Finally, he turned away, striding across the parking lot. He must have seen her in the store earlier.

Christie turned to the young woman. "Thanks. I appreciate your help."

"Us gals got to stick together. Lots of crazies out there right now. And you know what they say, one good turn deserves another."

"Yep. Thanks again."

"Y'all too. Have a blessed day." She moved on down the row toward her vehicle. Christie sat in her truck for a minute. First Susan, and now Cal. She just hoped the third time wouldn't mean harm.

~

Christie drove home and put away her

groceries and changed into riding boots before heading back down to the barn. Champ neighed when he saw her, and she stroked his muzzle. He followed her over to the area where she kept all her grooming tools. Grabbing the curry comb, she made her way down Champ's neck and shoulder before starting toward his withers and back. The simple movements allowed her mind to calm, and she spent time working the left side all the way down to his hocks before finishing that side and moving around to the right-hand side. Completing the task, she hauled the wool pad and saddle over and affixed it to him with the straps.

Climbing up into the saddle, she walked him out of the barn and out toward the property. The pair meandered past the scrub oak, taking a familiar trail that cut through the middle of the land. She was thankful for this time to get away and be alone with her thoughts. After a couple of hours, she was ready to return home. She pulled up in front of the horse trough so Champ could drink while she retrieved the sweat brush and hoof pick. She laid out all the items and went to bring Champ inside, where she removed the saddle and pad before working through his brushing.

It felt good to physically expend some labor, as it seemed to help regulate her emotional and mental state. She certainly felt calmer now that she'd taken time out to spend time riding Champ. The incident with Cal hadn't seemed that bad while it was happening, but she realized her tight shoulders and shallower breathing were telling her a different story of its effect on her. Leading Champ toward the corral, she ensured his feed tray was full of hay. Then she made her way back to the house.

A nice hot shower followed by dinner and vegging in front of the television would relax her even more. Inside her house, she allowed the hot spray of the shower to ease her tired muscles. Finally forcing herself to leave its warm delight, she toweled off before dressing in a pair of leggings, a warm sweatshirt, and fuzzy socks.

She'd put the frozen dinner in the microwave and set to adding a few logs to the woodstove when her phone rang.

An unknown number. Maybe it was Susan calling again. No, this was a different number. Still, she answered it.

"Hello?"

"Christie, please. Don't get involved."

"Abby! Where are you?"

"I can't say. But stay out of it. I don't want you hurt."

"Abby—"

The line had gone dead.

So much for all the self-care she'd done earlier. Christie felt the tension return to her body and her mind raced with what this meant.

What should she do with this information? She could call the deputy, but she wasn't even sure that they'd open a file on it. Plus, she really didn't have much to say, except this was the third time someone had told her to back off. Maybe it was for the best. If Abby killed Dax, the last thing Christie would want to do would be help a murderer escape justice. She stared at the phone for a while before picking it up.

Calling the number, she waited as it rang and rang. Abby wasn't answering.

Frustrated at not knowing where Abby was or why she'd called, she pounded the couch cushion with her hand. Had Abby called because she was concerned for Christie's welfare or threatening her? The call had been so quick it could have been either one, though it didn't seem like she was threatening Christie. None of this made sense.

Christie finished putting the kindling in the wood stove, watching as the flames caught the dry wood. The microwave dinged, letting her know the food was ready.

She grabbed it and switched on the TV, but her mind couldn't focus on any show. What she needed to do was step back and look at it from a different angle. But how could she do it?

The sun had set and while the house felt cozy with its blazing fire, it wasn't as comforting as it normally was. Of all the things that Christie felt were true now, it was that Dax didn't die accidentally. Someone had killed him.

The question was who and why?

CHAPTER SIXTEEN

Christie awoke the next morning with a renewed sense of focus. She needed to give more attention to the work at the rescue and leave all the craziness with Abby behind. There wasn't anything that she could do, though she was still debating on speaking to Deputy Graves about the incident with Cal along with the call from Abby.

Lana met her as she drove into the parking lot.

"Hey you. Long night?"

"What makes you say that?"

"You look like you didn't get enough sleep. Though maybe you need to learn better makeup tips for hiding the bruising."

Christie's fingers went to the side of her face as she touched it softly. "You know me and makeup. Not really my forte."

Lana grinned. "I can help you, but I doubt you need or want it. You're naturally hot."

"Yeah, that's me. Hot. From sweating out here

even in the cooler temps."

"So, spill. What's the real reason, then?" Lana asked.

"It's all the craziness with Abby's disappearance and everything else. Come on up to my office and I'll fill you in."

"Be glad to. Right now, I have to go meet all the new volunteers and show them around."

"Try not to scare them off." Christie replied.

Lana laughed, "Funny. You know me. Tough but fair."

"More like push-over."

"You got me. I'll stop in, say, thirty minutes. That work?"

"Perfect. I'll put on a fresh pot of coffee. Plus, I also want to go over the board's approval for the various budget items."

"Okay. See you in a few." Lana waved as she strode toward the group of people standing next to the barn doors.

Christie waved, and a few of the people returned the wave, while others faced away, looking into the barn. After making her way to the conference room where they kept the coffee, she took in a deep whiff of the ground beans. Scooping them into the pot, she hit the on switch and sat down to wait for Lana to arrive. While she waited, she took some time to check the rescue's social media, liking some posts of clients with the horses, while adding a word or two to some comments. She'd finished typing, 'Thanks to all our wonderful volunteers' when Lana arrived.

Christie stood and poured the hot, steaming coffee into two mugs with Horse Haven's logo on them. A gift from a local potter. She handed one cup to Lana before she doctored the brew with some cream.

Lana took a sip and sighed. "Ah, I needed that this morning."

"Everything okay?" Christie asked.

"Yes, though it was more work getting the volunteers briefed and started on the work for today."

Christie cupped the coffee mug with both hands. "I keep saying that you need to delegate that to others."

"I know. But I enjoy meeting them and I also want them to know that the work they are doing is serious. The animals depend on them, as do we."

"I get it. I'm trying to get better of giving more to Rene and others on staff, but I like to know what's going on, so I feel informed."

Lana scooted her chair closer. "Now, what's the scoop?"

"Abby called me."

"What? That's surprising. But good news, right? It means that nothing bad happened. At least to her."

"Yes, but something still feels off. I don't know if she was worried about my involvement or steering me away from investigating further by her low-key threats."

"As long as they don't put a stop to that check, I'm good with whatever she does."

"Ha. Ha. I think that could be another reason I'm a bit concerned about everything to do with her and Dax. If it turns out she killed Dax or had a hand in it, or if something else is going on, that could be bad publicity for the rescue. I don't want that happening. Better to return the check than have to deal with bad exposure tied to something nefarious."

"Oh, nefarious. Big word."

Christie swatted at her as Lana continued after a moment's pause, "I don't see that, but it's certainly something to consider. What if the money was drug money and they're really crime bosses who moved here to escape the people hunting for them?"

Christie raised an eyebrow and made a face. "Seriously? You've been watching way too many crime shows."

Lana raised her hand. "Guilty as charged."

"I was thinking of letting Deputy Graves know she called since he went out to the house, plus let him know about Cal."

Lana drank from her mug before replying, "He's that tall deputy with the cool green eyes."

Christie stared at Lana. "You've been paying attention to the deputy enough to know his eye color? Interesting."

Lana made a face. "It's nothing. Now stay focused. What about Cal?"

"Oh, I forgot to tell you. He threatened me, too."

"Geez. What have you done to deserve all this focus?"

"I don't know, but I'm getting a bit tired about it."

Lana stood and walked over to the sink. She washed out her cup and set it on the dish drainer. "It'll work out. It always does. Now I need to get back to work. Want to come over for dinner after church Sunday?"

"Sure. Sounds good. Let me ask Pop. Although, who am I kidding? All you have to say is 'free grub' and he's there."

Lana opened the door out to the hallway. She stepped out, then called over her shoulder. "Invite Bryson too. I always make enough for an army, so it's easier to do leftovers for the week."

Christie waved. "Will do."

After refilling her mug, she made her way back to her office. Setting the cup down, she searched in her bag for a business card Deputy Grimes had given her at Abby's house. Finding the card, she punched in his number. After a few rings, he answered.

"Grimes."

Christie relayed the info about Abby and Cal. After saying she didn't want to press any charges against Cal, they concluded their discussion. A thought came to Christie.

"Deputy Grimes?"

"Yes?"

"Are you available for lunch on Sunday?"

There was a moment of silence. Christie continued. "Lana, the vet here at the rescue is making lunch and I'm coming with my father and my fiancé, Bryson. Thought you might enjoy a home-cooked meal."

Christie had noticed that he wore no wedding band on his finger, but that didn't mean anything. She better cover all her bases. "And of course, your wife and family, too."

"I'm not married."

Christie smiled to herself. "Well, the

invitation stands. I'll be making my Armadillo Pie too and I think Lana will have a brisket she cooked overnight."

"Not sure about that pie, but I've heard you make some of the best pies in Comfort so I'm willing to give it a shot. Plus, I don't turn down home-cooked brisket. I think I can swing it. What time?"

"Say one?"

"Okay. Text me the address."

Christie answered. "Will do it right after we get off the call." Her fingers were already typing in the address.

The call ended, and Christie smiled with satisfaction. If Lana had wanted to play matchmaker for Christie, now she was going to get a taste of her own medicine.

~

Sunday arrived and Bryson drove Christie from church over for lunch. It was hard to think of it as Lana's place now, as it had always been Curtis's for as long as Christie could recall. But with Lana and her kids taking over the big house and Curtis moving into a smaller tiny home on the property, the life of a young family had transformed the house into a home of constant movement. Curtis had parked his truck over by his place and was striding over to the big house. While they'd said they'd drive Pop, he was stubborn enough to want his own vehicle so he could leave and head home whenever he wanted.

Christie had brought the pies over last night, so she wouldn't have to go home to pick them up. She wore a turquoise dress with a brown belt, a brown jacket, and boots.

Bryson pulled over next to a stand of small trees. "Before I forget. You look lovely today."

Christie blushed. "Thanks. Now let's get inside so I can see if Lana needs any help before Deputy Grimes arrives." Christie had told Lana about inviting Deputy Grimes today, so it wouldn't be a surprise when he arrived. But Lana had shaken her finger at Christie, spouting, "Now don't you get any ideas in your head!"

"Me? Never." She'd winked.

Bryson laid his hand lightly on the small of

her back as they met up with Curtis.

"How's it going there, fella? Didn't get a chance to talk to ya earlier."

Bryson smiled and shook Curtis's weathered hand. "All good, Mr. Altgelt."

"I don't know about you, but I'm sure hankering for some of Lana's good cooking. Let's not dilly dally out here. " He walked on ahead of the couple.

Inside, they were met with the savory smells from the kitchen. "Smells delicious, darlin." Curtis sat down in a recliner in front of the television, switching it to a football game pre-event. Christie knew that Curtis and Pop would be eating dessert in front of the television. The kids were off with friends, so it would be the six of them for lunch.

Lana came to the table carrying a bowl of heaping mashed potatoes, rivers of yellow melted butter sneaking down the sides. Christie moaned. Why did food have to taste so good? The temptation to stick her finger in the fluffy goodness was only restrained by her maturity.

Lana still wore the skirt and top she'd had on at church, only switching out her heels for a pair of fuzzy pink slippers. She beckoned Christie to help lay out the rest of the items on the table. They'd finished putting the dishes in their places when there was a knock on the door. It was Deputy Grimes.

Curtis yelled, "Door's open. Come in!"

Grimes entered the house, and his towering, muscular build took up a lot of the doorway. In place of his normal khaki colored uniform, he wore a red and black plaid button-down shirt and starched jeans. He had on black Justin boots. In keeping with his role and being used to carrying, his holster sat snug against his side. In his hands, he bore a bouquet, but they weren't normal grocery store fare. It comprised zinnias and other flowers. He handed the bouquet to Lana. "These are for you. They're from my garden. Thanks for the lunch invitation."

She smiled up at him. "Well, you can thank Christie for that, but I'm glad you decided to accept. I'll just put these in some water."

Lana rushed out of the room, flushed, as the men began talking about last week's turnovers and touchdowns. Christie strolled into the kitchen, where Lana was pulling a crystal vase from the cabinet.

"It's just lunch, Lana."

The young woman let out a breath. "You're right. I don't know why I got so flustered out there." She poured water into the vase.

"You weren't. It may have felt like it, but you were fine. Better than fine. Perfect."

Lana snipped off the stem of a flower stalk before adding it to the vase of water. "I just don't want him getting the wrong idea."

"That you like him? No man is going to be upset by thinking that a woman finds him attractive. You do, don't you?"

Lana chuckled as she snipped another flower. "Yes. I've spoken to him before, I don't know—"

"For everything, there is a season." Christie replied. Lana's first husband had died serving his country overseas. Though years had passed, Lana and her children still missed their husband and father. It was time to allow someone to come in and help mend that gap. Christie hugged her friend. "I love you."

"I love you too. Even if you are a meddler."

"Kettle. Black. Again, it's not anything huge."

"You're right. Just lunch." Lana finished arranging the flowers before taking them out and placing them on the sideboard next to the table. "Let's eat!" Curtis turned off the television to Pop's dismay, but that was a strict rule in Lana's home. No TV on during the time they were eating. The exception was made for Friday movie nights, when one of the kids was sick, or for today, during dessert.

The meal went well, and everyone laughed as Pop and Curtis shared humorous story after story. Deputy Grimes shared some stories as well and revealed his name to be Drake. Finally, Curtis and Pop glanced at their watches, signaling the game was on.

"All right. The no TV time is expired."

Pop and Curtis immediately moved to the chairs in front of the screen.

"Christie, can you help me clear the table?"

"Certainly." She grabbed some plates while Bryson and Drake picked up the larger serving containers, walking them into the kitchen. After the table had been cleared, they decided they'd wait a bit to eat dessert. Lana put on the coffee pot in case anyone wanted a cup.

"How about a game of dominoes?" Bryson asked.

"Or we could play a game the kids like." Lana replied.

Christie responded, "What is it?"

"Settlers of Catan."

"That's a great game." Drake said.

"How do you know it?"

"I volunteer with a program that is mentoring a boy whose father's no longer in his life. We play it when we're not outdoors. I like spending time outside with him as it makes it easier to talk about things on his mind."

"Oh, Trey would love that."

Grimes said, "Who's Trey?"

"He's my son. I also have a daughter, Allie."

"That's wonderful." Grimes picked up the board game as Lana met Christie's glance.

Deputy Grimes held up the board, "So, this one?"

"I'm game." Bryson replied.

Christie nodded. "Me too."

Lana retrieved the board game from Grimes, and they started setting up the hexagonal squares. "Just so y'all know, I'm highly competitive."

Drake chuckled. "That makes two of us."

"Sounds like you two would make a good team." Bryson responded.

Drake focused on the game pieces while Lana blushed a bright red.

CHAPTER SEVENTEEN

Monday rolled around and Christie forced herself to get up earlier than usual to get chores done. One thing she hated about the changing seasons was having to rise while it was still dark. The alarm went off again as she rolled over, pulling the pillow over her head.

Whose dumb idea was it to set the alarm for so early?

She threw off the covers, forcing herself to leave the warm comfort of her bed, trudging over to the bathroom where she flipped on the overhead light. Last night she'd prepared for the morning by having her clothes ready to go. Pulling her hair back into a ponytail, she brushed her teeth, rinsing her face with cold, bracing water to help her wake up even more. She downed a glass of water she'd prepared before pulling on a long-sleeve t-shirt and a pair of comfortable, faded work jeans. Christie made her way to the front door where her boots were set out along with a Nalgene bottle full of water. She grabbed the baseball cap with the attached light on it, switching it on as she settled it on her head. Finally, she pocketed her phone in the pocket of her fleece vest before heading out the door. The fall air was crisp as she made her way down the stairs and over to the barn, the edges of the pink sunset noticeably toward the east.

Champ was in his stall, so she greeted him and led him out to the corral where she filled his feed tray and made sure he had fresh water. After she'd spent some time with him, she trekked over to the barn. Flipping on the overhead lights helped to limit the gloom in the barn where the cool darkness still hid from the rising sun. While she was used to working alone without feeling spooked, she cranked up the portable radio with oldies but goodies tunes.

Geez, you know you're growing older when they call the songs you grew up with oldies.

Her lightweight vest was soon removed, and her sleeves pushed up to her elbows as she mucked out Champ's stall, placing the spent straw and manure in a wheelbarrow that would be added to the pile out back for their spring garden. This year she hadn't spent much time tending the garden or doing any canning, as the rescue took up so much of her time. Even though it was more mental than physical work at the rescue, she often found herself drained when she arrived home. Canning was such a major process. Though Pop had the canning kitchen at his place which did make the job easier. She'd need to set aside a long weekend to do put up some food and prepare some piecrusts she could freeze for the holidays. In some ways, it reminded her of her mother and those memories were a comfort after her mom had left this earth for heaven.

A noise made her glance toward the front of the barn. She rested her hand on the pitchfork, listening. Maybe Champ had hit something. She peered out of the stall, but all was quiet. Most likely, it was something on the radio. She set the pitchfork along the wall, grabbing the handles of the wheelbarrow with her stained leather gloves.

The wheel squeaked as she made her way down the center aisle of the barn.

Crack.

She swung around. "Who's there?"

No answer.

Christie had moved far enough away from the stall that she wouldn't be able to grab the pitchfork.

A shadow passed by the open barn door. Christie moved so that the wheelbarrow was facing toward the door. If nothing else, she'd be able to use it as some protection if it was deer or other wild animal. While not common, there had been a few sightings of wild hogs, though Champ would have been more active in the corral.

The overhead lighting fell on the person who entered the barn. The person wore a bulky Carhartt jacket, a baseball cap, and a pair of sunglasses. But Christie knew immediately who it was.

"Hello, Abby."

"Not a great disguise, then?" Abby laughed.

"We all tend to have mannerisms, even our

walk, which gives us away."

Abby removed the glasses, placing them in the jacket's pocket. She pulled off the cap, running her fingers through the short, cropped hair, now a chocolate-brown tone in place of the long blond hair.

"Oh, you cut your hair off. Wait a minute. Were you in the new batch of volunteers the other day?"

Abby nodded. "Yes, I figured the best place to hide was in plain sight. Plus, I know people tend to talk too. I figured I'd get at least some info on what's been happening." She sighed. "I know you have questions, too."

"Yes. Quite a few, actually. But one in particular. " Christie hadn't moved toward the young woman.

Abby sighed. "I'm tired. I can't keep this up and I don't know where to turn. I thought that things would settle down if I made myself scarce for a bit, but he just won't stop."

"Wait, what do you mean won't. You mean wouldn't, don't you?"

"No. I mean what I said."

Christie pulled off her gloves but stayed in between the handles of the wheelbarrow. She had never thought Abby was a killer, but she'd been wrong before. Better to have this between them.

"Let me get this straight. You're talking about Dax and his behavior before his death. Correct?

Abby's hands fidgeted with the ball cap. "No. I'm talking about Cal."

"Cal? What's he got to do with this?"

"He's blackmailing me."

Christie stared at Abby, trying to wrap her mind around what Abby'd just said. "Just go to the police."

"I can't. They'll find out the truth."

"That you killed Dax?" Christie's back grew cold with the sweat from earlier. She wished she had her vest right now, especially since it held her cell phone.

Abby broke down crying. "I didn't kill Dax."

Susan stepped out of the shadows. "I did."

CHAPTER EIGHTEEN

Christie thought fast. Susan was so close to Abby there was no way that she could reach the young woman in time. She could sprint for her phone. But that wouldn't do any good if Susan had any weapon. Her hands didn't appear to hold anything, but she had it in the pocket of her large coat.

But it was Abby that surprised Christie when she fell sobbing into Susan's arms. It made no sense. Yet something had niggled at her mind the first time she'd seen Susan at Dax's funeral.

"You're not Abby's sister-in-law. You're her mother."

Susan wiped the tears from her eyes, sniffling. "You got me."

"I have to say, this is getting weirder and weirder. Why all the subterfuge about being her sister-in-law?"

"Because, technically, I am."

Christie crossed her arms. "Okay, I know it's

early, but this is getting increasingly difficult to wrap my head around what you're saying. How in the world can you be her mother- and sister-in-law? That's, um--"

"I think the word you're looking for is 'weird.' And I know what you're thinking, but it's not like that at all. Abby's husband is, or was, my stepbrother on my mother's side. Well, there's definitely a story that I want to hear about that, but first, there's the issue of you killing Dax."

Susan broke down sobbing. "I didn't mean to do it. I didn't mean to kill anyone. I only meant to put Cal out of commission so he couldn't work at the winery anymore and leave Abby alone. Cal had goaded Dax, making him think that Abby was cheating on him."

Christie thought back to Dax's outburst the first time she'd gone over to Fat Cat. "What have you done?" he'd screamed at her. Looking back, she realized that his face at the time wasn't one of anger but of hurt and betrayal.

She spoke to them. "Cal had been trying to cause a division between you and Dax. What purpose would that serve?"

"The only thing I can think of is that he was trying to cause so many problems for us with the winery and our relationship, that we'd forget moving forward and sell out to Roland Lewis."

A deep male voice spoke. "But you didn't. You just kept working it out. You and your 'don't worry, honey, it will all be okay' mantra. I was sick of it."

Susan engulfed Abby in her embrace as they moved away from Cal. "I wouldn't do that if I were you. Not a step farther." He pulled a gun from behind his back. Motioning with it, he instructed, "All of you. Get over together."

Christie thought fast. The only thing between her and him was the wheelbarrow. "I'm not moving." She stated firmly, though she heard her voice shaking.

He glared at her but said nothing. "You two. Go over by her."

Susan and Abby scurried over toward where Christie stood. If they could call for the sheriff's department, they'd have a chance. If she could only get to her vest.

"I'm getting cold. Can I get my vest?"

"You must think I'm stupid." He walked over and pulled her phone from the pocket before throwing it down on the dirt floor and crushing it under his boot. "You two. Throw me your phones!"

Abby threw her phone toward him, but Susan responded, "I left it in my car."

He motioned. "Take off your coat. And do it slowly."

As Susan pulled her arm from one sleeve, Cal whipped around as they heard a voice. Susan had made a call and dropped her phone, scooting it toward bales of hay while Cal had been watching me. A light came on outside and it was enough of a distraction that Christie grabbed the wheelbarrow, rushing toward Cal. He only had time to glance back as she hit him full on just above the knees, causing him to crumple to the ground. The gun flew from his hand, skidding across the dirt floor. Christie lifted the wheelbarrow, dumping the manure and spent straw on top of Cal.

Deputy Grimes stepped into view. "Great. Now my cruiser's going to smell like you-know-what."

Christie burst out laughing as Susan and Abby hugged her. "You saved us."

"No. Susan did."

~

Christie rang the doorbell at Abby's house. Susan answered, gathering Christie up in a hug and offering her hand to Bryson, who carried one of Christie's pies, this one a warm caramel apple.

"Come in. Come in." She opened the door wider so that Christie and Bryson could enter.

Abby made her way toward them, wiping her hands on a dish towel. "Thanks for coming. I figured we owed you 'the rest of the story' now that Cal's confessed to Dax's murder and is in jail pending trial. But first, let's enjoy a nice lunch and talk about lighter things."

Christie handed the warm pie to Susan. "That sounds wonderful."

As Susan took the pie to the kitchen, Abby led

them toward a dining room which opened on the back terrace. "It's such a lovely day I thought we'd sit outside, but we can always sit in the dining room. I'm still getting used to the climate here but wanted to take advantage of the warmer weather while it's still around."

"I love that idea." Christie responded.

Bryson walked behind Christie as they made their way outdoors. "This is nice. I love the way the pool is accessible, but also the layout back here."

"Yes, Dax did a good job on the landscape for the back. I'm staying here for now, but I plan on selling."

Bryson said, "Just curious. How much you asking?"

Abby smiled, "Well, if you're interested, I happen to know the owner and we could work out a good deal."

He glanced over at Christie, her face an expression of surprise. "Well, I'll keep that in mind."

Christie chimed in. "Quick question. When I

came over that day, were you hiding out in the shed?"

"You caught me. I thought at first you might be Cal. I didn't have anywhere else to go."

Christie nodded. "That makes sense why your purse and keys were still there." She turned to Susan. "You heard me and distracted me from checking it out?"

"Not exactly. When you called the sheriff's office, I had to act quickly, as I wasn't sure they'd search the shed."

"Wait a minute. So, when we were talking, Abby sneaked around the side and got into the back seat of your car?"

Abby set a casserole dish of scalloped potatoes down on the table. "Yes. I'm a pretty quick runner and since I'm small, I was able to get in her car without being noticed."

"But I looked in the back seat. There was a blanket, but you weren't under it."

Abby nodded. "You're right. I was in the big box in the back of the SUV. The blanket was if I didn't have time to make it back there. You almost caught me if it weren't for Susan pulling your attention back to what was happening."

Susan appeared, holding a long platter that held a poached salmon with lemon slices on top and decorated with lemon wedges and dill along the sides. "I hope you all like salmon."

"Looks wonderful. Need help with anything else?" Christie asked.

"Bryson, would you give me a hand?" Abby asked, leaving Susan and Christie alone.

Susan took a moment before speaking. "I'm sorry for all the subterfuge. But I was so worried about Abby. I didn't know who I could trust. I'm ashamed to say that you received quite a bit of the anger I was feeling."

"No apology necessary. If I were in your shoes, I would have felt the same way. I'm just glad that Cal confessed, but I am looking forward to hearing that story."

Abby and Bryson arrived at the table, Abby carrying a large mixed salad and a bottle of vinaigrette and Bryson holding a dish of butter and a loaf of warm, crusty bread.

Christie looked at the dishes. "This looks delightful. I should have made my Armadillo Pie instead of apple."

"Oh, no. It will be perfect. Plus, I love apple pie." Susan replied.

The luncheon was enjoyable as the group listened to stories from Bryson and Christie about growing up around Comfort, and the two ladies also shared some of their own tales. As they sat back in their seats, satiated by the food and the warm sunshine on their backs, the mood turned more serious.

Christie broke the silence. "If you'd rather not talk about it, I'll respect it. But I'm wondering about your relationship."

Susan stared off in the distance for a moment before composing herself. Her voice was soft as she recounted her story. "I was really young when I found out I was pregnant with Abby. My father was extremely upset, as probably any parent would be in that situation. But it grew worse when I wouldn't name the father. What we'd done was wrong, but we were wrong for each other. My father was livid. When I said that I would bring the baby up on my own, well, it all went downhill from there. He forged documents and paid off some people to have my baby adopted."

Susan turned to Abby. "I would have never left you willingly. My father had power and pull, and most of all, money. My mother didn't know what he'd done either. It was the end of their marriage and even though we both begged my father to tell us who had adopted you, he refused. He died a few years after they divorced, but I never stopped looking for you." She reached over and grasped Abby's hand in hers. "That's why it was such a miracle when I found you."

Christie leaned closer. "When Abby married your step-brother?"

"Yes. My mother remarried a man with two sons and a daughter. I was only there for a short while before heading off to college, but I'd become good friends with the son. We were about the same age and had a lot of similar interests. Out of the blue, he says he's met this young woman, but he's concerned about the age difference between them."

Susan stopped for a moment. "I warned him about age differences. But if I'd have told him not to pursue it, my entire life would be different. Instead, I asked if he loved her and did she love him too. He said that they'd both been concerned about the age gap and had even broken up, but they continued to be drawn back to one another. He felt God had brought Abby to him." She paused a moment. "I laugh about that now. There was definitely some things going on beyond the earthly realm. Now I realize that Abby needed me.

She paused. "Anyway, they gave up fighting against their feelings for one another and eloped. The first time I saw Abby, I knew. People would even say things like, 'your daughter, or 'your mom'. We'd laugh, but I had to know for sure. I had a DNA test done on both of us. It was a match."

Christie realized that was why Susan looked so familiar. The resemblance when they were together was evident.

Abby's eyes sparkled with tears. "I loved my

mother and father who brought me up, and when I was older, she told me I was adopted. I always wondered about my birth parents but had no way to find them. I certainly did not know that anything like this would happen."

Christie added, "Which is why there's that old saying about there being nothing a mother wouldn't do for her child."

Susan nodded. "I wasn't sure I should tell Abby that I was her mother. To say it was a strange situation is an understatement. But then, Rob was killed in a terrible accident. I knew that was my chance to give Abby what was rightfully hers."

"What do you mean?" Abby gawked.

"Rob didn't have any money. I mean, yes, he had money. But not like the money on your grandfather's side of the family. When Rob died, I contacted a lawyer and had them send you money like it was a settlement from insurance."

"It wasn't?"

Susan shook her head. "No. I wanted to make up for the past, though I'm so thankful for your adoptive parents. I couldn't have asked for better people to bring up my daughter."

"Wait a minute. Some years back, they heard they'd inherited a place in Hawaii. Don't tell me that was you too?" Abby gasped.

Susan shrugged her shoulders with a big grin on her face.

Abby sat back, stunned. "I can't believe this. Every month, my bank account had more funds deposited. That must mean I'm a …millionaire?"

Susan stuck her hair behind her ear. "Technically, with the corporation's assets, landholdings, and other securities, change that from an m to a b."

Abby's mouth, along with Christie's dropped open. "A billionaire?"

"I know it's a lot to take in. Turns out I'm pretty good at investing and business, along with supporting entrepreneurs. I once gave a friend from college a hundred bucks to help him get started on an idea he had with computers."

"Whoa. I can't believe this." Abby rose from her seat, pacing around. "What company?"

"Um, let's chat on that later. As for now, how about some of that 'apple' pie?"

230

CHAPTER NINETEEN

After the group enjoyed pie and coffee, Christie came back to the recent events. "Are you ready now to share about what's been going on here in the last few weeks?"

Susan nodded. "Abby, why don't you start and then I'll chime in."

"Sure." Abby took a deep breath. "I'd found out about Susan being my mom some time before we moved here. We'd started chatting over the computer and the phone. When she told me she had a conference she was attending in San Antonio, I invited her to stay with me and Dax."

Susan picked up. "Dax was a good man, but I could tell he was troubled. Sadly, we have so many veterans that feel they need to be strong and won't reach out for the help they need. I was worried about him, but not surprisingly, I was more worried about Abby, especially when she'd come home with the bruises on her arms."

Abby interjected. "Dax caused the bruises,

but it was due to him catching me as I started to fall. I didn't want to say he did it, as it would give people the wrong idea. It really was because of working in the winery at such a fast pace and grueling schedule."

Abby sat down in her chair before continuing. "I thought I was doing a good thing a few months ago when I ran across Cal. They'd been friends in school and joined up together. I figured that it would be good for Dax to have someone he could talk to about what he was facing with his issues from the tours. Of course, finding out he had diabetes at least gave me some idea about the huge mood swings he was experiencing. He'd be so nice to others and then if his blood sugar dropped, you never knew when he would lash out over something insignificant. I finally started to see the signs and could help him eat something or just to know to stay out of his way for a bit. But then things started going wrong. First, it was little minor things and then bigger things. Sometimes it was only a setback of minutes, but soon it was hours and days. Dax grew increasingly upset. I asked him to call the VA and get some counseling or a check-up, but his focus was on the opening. I couldn't shake him off it."

She bowed her head. "I then made the biggest mistake of all. I didn't know that Cal was behind everything. But all along, he'd been leading me down a path he'd created. He knew that I'd seek him out and talk to him about Dax. Of course, as soon as he'd see Dax, he'd place his hand on my arm, or give me a hug. At the time, I didn't realize what he was doing. I thought he was simply trying to be kind. In reality, he was putting thoughts in Dax's mind that we were having an affair. Cal wanted to split us up. It drove Dax even more into depression. He's the one who destroyed our bedroom, looking for something to confirm my affair with Cal."

Abby stopped to compose herself as tears glistened in her eyes. "I would never have cheated on Dax. I loved him. Even with all his problems, I knew that we had to work through it, and I had to support him and continue to advise him to get therapy. When I heard what you all were doing with the horses, I thought I could get involved that way and then introduce him to the idea of helping others first. Then he might see that it would help him too."

"That's smart. I can't imagine dealing with what you've done day after day. It would be like walking on eggshells all the time."

Abby wiped her eyes, and using a napkin, blew her nose. "I meant what I said when we married. For better or worse." She laughed. "Of course, when you're saying those words, you're only focused on the better and richer portion. Now, I'll never have the chance to tell him how much I loved him and how Cal had been trying to split us apart." She broke down again as Susan gathered the sobbing young woman in her arms.

Returning to her seat, Susan started the story, "During this time, I could feel the tension and asked Abby what I could do to help. She told me she suspected Cal of causing problems instead of helping. She was going to tell Dax to fire him. Dax wouldn't tell Abby what had happened on their tour, but he owed Cal or said he did. But the thought of an affair was causing a lot of friction. They got into a fight and Cal got hurt. The two acted as if it were rough housing that had gotten out of hand, but things were definitely spiraling out of control at that point. Abby was upset because Dax felt he couldn't let him go then. Plus, he knew if Cal left, it would cause more delays. I overheard him telling Abby he'd sack Cal once they'd finished with the last batches."

"I stayed away as much as I could, and I guess Susan could see how upset I was about the whole situation. Not only was Cal trying to sabotage the winery's operations, but he was trying to destroy our marriage. It finally came to a head recently when I came home, and Cal was sitting on the lounger in the back. He acted like he owned the place. I told him to leave, but he wouldn't go. Kept saying that Dax wasn't good enough for someone like me. That he and I could have a good life together. To be honest, if Susan hadn't arrived, I hate to think what he might have tried." Abby shivered.

Susan picked up her glass and took a swallow

of iced tea as Abby spoke. She set it down. "That's when I knew I had to do something. Cal was growing more dangerous by the day. I refused to let anything happen to her after finally finding her. Abby has this thing about dental floss. The last vat had a catwalk at the top and she'd told me that a few of the workers had tripped on a step toward the top. It had some kind of flaw or something that threw off your balance. They planned on getting rid of it after they'd finished that batch. Anyway, they were going to get rid of it and put in a new one. But I had an idea. I knew Cal knew about that step, so he'd be focused on it, but not the next one up. I figured he'd let his guard down after bypassing the problem step. I could tie the floss across the upper step, and it would trip him, and he'd fall against the railing and the top bar. I figured it would be enough to get him out of the picture, if only for a day or two."

Susan clinched her hands, before rubbing them together. "Of course, as soon as I'd fixed it, I realized what a horrible thing I'd done. I berated myself over it and I rang up Abby and told her.

She was already on her way to your place, but she'd stop by on the way back. Dax had promised he would take off sometime that day. So, it didn't seem that we needed to get in any big hurry to go over and remove it from the stair."

Abby interjected. "Maybe Cal showed up and saw it, thinking I'd done it. Now I don't know if he thought I was going after Dax, but he thought it was a fantastic opportunity to get rid of Dax. He told me he cut the floss off the stairs and hid it away. Then he called Dax to see if he was coming to the winery. From that point, I don't know what happened except that he lured Dax up to the catwalk." She swallowed against the emotion building up in her throat. "Poor Dax. He thought Cal was his friend. Of course, he didn't tell me this until later when he started blackmailing me."

Bryson glanced at Christie, and she knew he was thinking the same thing—'With friends like that, you don't need enemies.'

Christie added, "So what happened after you found Dax?"

"I couldn't find the floss that Susan had told

me about. I searched, but it was nowhere to be found. Then I wondered if Dax had taken it. But it was a day later when Cal showed up at the house, telling me he knew I'd tried to kill Dax and he'd helped me get rid of him. Now we could be together. I thought I'd throw up with what he'd told me. I didn't know what to do."

"You couldn't share that you were innocent without pointing the finger at Susan." Bryson said.

"Exactly. I even thought of offering him money to keep him quiet."

Susan interrupted. "I knew that wouldn't work. We were dealing with a maniac. He wanted Abby, and he wouldn't stop until he had her. That's when I told Abby she needed to 'disappear' for a while until we could figure out the best way forward. If nothing else, it would give us some time. We drove over to Kerrville, and she had her hair cut and dyed. But we needed to keep her around people. That's when she said she could volunteer at the rescue. I figured Cal would be watching to see where I went so Abby would hitch a ride into Boerne, I'd park at HEB and go shopping while leaving the car open. She'd sneak in while I was inside and once we got to the house, I'd make sure we weren't being watched before she'd sneak inside."

"Geez, it sounds like something out of a made for tv movie. Ya'll really thought of everything."

"Well, not everything. We got worried Cal might come after you, thinking you were sheltering Abby."

"Ah, so that explains the 'back-off' call." Christie said.

"Yes. I knew he was dangerous. Susan decided we had to tell the truth. It was the only way forward. But we wanted to let you know first. I didn't know that she'd called Deputy Grimes and let him know to meet us at your place. We knew Cal was following her. We did not know he'd be there so early in the morning, though."

Bryson added, "He must have been parked out from the house. He knew you'd lead him to Abby eventually."

Susan nodded. "Sadly, yes. We'd done so well

until that point. If nothing else, I have the money for good lawyers. And at this point, no charges have been brought against me or Abby."

"We'll pray they never do." Christie said. "What about the winery?"

"Susan had an idea and I think we're going to be moving in a different direction." Abby glanced over at Susan, who nodded agreement. Her voice was animated as she spoke. "The winery was going to take such a long time and there were so many things involved. Truth be told, that was really Dax's dream. We discussed moving forward or selling the property. We went through a bunch of concepts. But then we just knew it when we came up with the idea."

"What then?" Christie asked.

"Fat Cat balsamic vinegar and other vinegars like apple cider vinegar. Obviously, we aren't growing apples, but we have the Trebbiano grape vines. I think that may have been why we were having some difficulty with the production."

"What about Roland Lewis and wanting to buy the property?"

Abby winked at Susan. "Let's just say that he's spoken with Susan and there may be a business opportunity for him, so he's more open-minded now."

"It looks like things are going to move forward in a positive direction for you. So, what's next?"

"We want to make up for lost time of being apart all these years. Once everything gets settled with the court cases, we'll be heading over to Europe for a couple of months to do some sight-seeing."

Susan smiled as Abby added, "I'm looking forward to getting to know my mother."

CHAPTER TWENTY

Cal ended up confessing to Dax's death, stating that they had fought, and Dax had slipped, and hit his head. He'd run to get help but when he got back to Dax, he found him in the vat, dead. Whether that was the truth or not, Cal ended up accepting a plea deal for a shorter sentence, saving the long-drawn out ordeal of a trial for Abby and Susan. He also didn't bring up the dental floss Susan had strung across the stair as it would open him up to extortion and obstruction of justice charges. Learning that, Susan and Abby had felt relieved, but it came with a cost. Susan would have to see Cal. She agreed, deciding it was better to face him now than later.

Before he was transferred to Huntsville, Cal asked Abby for her forgiveness, saying that he only wanted to protect her. She refused to talk about it and once anything relating to the case was closed; the pair left for their trip to Europe. Susan had purchased a home in the Dominion so she could be closer to Abby. She'd invited Abby's adoptive parents to visit, and she and Abby's mom had hit it off right away.

Life had returned to the humdrum of work at the rescue, while Lana and Drake had dated for a while before Lana introduced him to Allie and Trey. Allie, already moving into her 'whatever' phase, didn't seem concerned about this new man in her mother's life while Trey had quickly warmed up to him. While Curtis had been a good male influence in the boy's life, Drake had taken it a step further with taking Trey fishing and spending lots of one-on-one time together. As Drake's influence took hold, Trey's grades had improved, and he'd taken to being more responsible.

As for Christie and Bryson, plans were forming for a wedding the following spring and Abby had offered her house for the reception venue. It was certainly large enough for the small wedding Christie envisioned.

It was nice that everything had finally settled

down again.

Christie loaded up some boxes into her truck that she was taking into the thrift store. She needed to think about making room for Bryson's stuff. And they'd begun to talk about building a place that didn't have stairs for their later years. The current cob house on stilts would be perfect for renting out to guests visiting the area.

Her phone rang. It was her dear friend, Orchid.

Orchid had been away for some months, speaking about her weaving and displaying her wares in many museums and art galleries across the country. Some days Christie would drive by Orchid's house with the latest artwork that Orchid had painted on it before she left. Stars decorated the top of the door in various shapes, with the background shade morphing from light to dark sky. A quote was placed in the middle of the door with the words, "I'll see you on the other side of the stars." At the bottom of the door, soft tones of pink, yellow, and orange signified the rising of the sun.

"Orchid! I'm so happy to hear from you. It's been ages. When did you get back into town?"

"Hello, my dear. I'm sorry I haven't reached out sooner. While I was away, a large tree branch fell onto my gazebo in the back."

Christie recalled the storm that had seen many tree branches falling down and causing a lot of clean-up. "Oh, sorry to hear that."

"It's fine. But when it fell, it caused some damage to the side of the gazebo. Since I'd been wanting to change it up, I figured this would be as good a time as any to do it." She sighed.

"What's the matter?"

"I need your help, Christie. They've found a body—well..."

"What?"

"Actually, they think it may be two bodies."

Christie leaned against the truck before breaking out into laughing hysterically.

"Christie, dear, are you all right?"

She fought to compose herself. "Yes, sorry. It hit me funny, that's all. I thought leaving the nursing profession would be the end of my having to deal with death all the time. Instead, it's like death has followed me home."

Orchid's melodious voice came over the speaker, "Maybe, it's that you went from attending people who needed your help in their last moments to helping people who have died receive the justice they deserve."

"I suppose. It's just been a bit weird. I should take up writing and change my name to Jessica Fletcher."

"Sometimes we use humor to get us through the tragedies of life. For whatever reason, you've been chosen to help bring closure. I'd like to help whoever these people are in my yard to receive the proper ending they deserve. And their families deserve."

Christie's ears perked at that last statement. It meant something to her. But what? "I'll be over in a little while. Pack a bag and you can stay with me."

"I already have that sorted, but I really want you here. I know that if anyone can figure out why there's two bodies in my backyard, it's you."

"Okay. Be over soon." Christie rang off and closed the truck bed. She climbed into the cab, sitting there for a moment in the stillness, taking in the information and the thoughts from Orchid.

Some memory was already tickling at the back of her mind just out of reach.

She glanced over to the empty passenger seat before stating, "Okay, death, let's crack this case."

~

Want to know when the next book, Death Wakes A Snake, will be coming out? You'll have access to some stories and excerpts only available to Vikki's cozy readers, along with monthly giveaways. So, what are ya waiting for? Sign up now! https://www.vikkiwalton.com/newsletter/

FROM THE AUTHOR

I hope you enjoyed reading Death Cracks The Case. Would you do me a huge favor and leave a written review on Bookbub, Goodreads, or your favorite book retailer? It helps other readers to know if this is a good fit for them and I deeply appreciate your taking the time to leave a review. Have you read my other books in this series or my other cozy mystery series?

A Taylor Texas Mystery Series

    Death Takes A Break

    Death Makes A Move

    Death Stakes A Claim

    Death Steals A Kiss

    Death Cracks The Case

    Death Wakes A Snake (next in series)

A Backyard Farming Mystery Series

    Chicken Culprit

Cordial Killing

Honey Homicide

Christmas Capers

Potager Plot

Duck Disaster

Fungi Foul Play (next in series; coming June 2023)

Viviane's Adventures Mystery Series

Hijinks in Ajijic (short story prequel)

Deception in Devon

Larceny in London (next in series)

It is often said that you don't write alone, and this is true. It takes a lot of people to assist in getting a book from idea to printed page. Even with lots of editing and formatting programs, and many eyes on the story, some things sneak through to the finished book. I hope you'll give me grace and I accept full responsibility for any errors you find in the book.

Want to learn about upcoming releases or promotions, giveaways, or just stuff in general? Then I urge you to sign up for my newsletter. I don't spam you all the time and will only send you emails once or twice a month. That's it. Sometimes if there are some great cozies from my author friends I want to share, you may get some extra emails, but those aren't all the time.

Go to my website to sign up.

www.vikkiwalton.com

You can also follow me on Bookbub at

https://www.bookbub.com/authors/vikki-walton

Happy Reading!

TEXAS ARMADILLO PIE RECIPE

A Texan take on the Arkansas Possum Pie, this pie can be made with any puddling flavor desired. Instructions included are for basic vanilla pudding and an option for chocolate. Though you can change it up by adding different flavors by replacing the vanilla in the basic pudding with such flavorings as almond, hazelnut, or coconut, or peppermint (for chocolate mint pie). A word of caution though—peppermint goes a long way, so combine the vanilla (1 ½ tsp) with a touch of peppermint (Tsp ¼ to ½).

Texas Armadillo Pie is made up for four layers. The bottom layer is the crust, the next layer is sweetened cream cheese, next is your pudding layer, topped with fresh whipped cream. Optional items are adding a sprinkling of chopped pecans, toasted coconut, chocolate shavings or sprinkles or if you want to forgo the whipped cream, you can add fruit.

Ingredients Required

Flour

Cornstarch

Salt

Sugar (white)

Sugar (brown)

Sugar (powdered)

Butter

Milk

Eggs

Cream Cheese

Heavy Cream (for cream cheese layer and if you're making whipped cream from scratch)

Pecans, chopped (For Texas Armadillo Pie use the Texas State Nut—the Pecan!.

Optional items:

Sprinkles

Coconut

Fruit or fruit zest

Tools Required:

Bowls for mixing and cooling

Pans

Whisk or fork, spatulas

Pie pan (9 inch)

Measuring cups and spoons

Hot pads or gloves

Whipped Cream Dispenser (if making fresh whipped cream)

Pie Crust (bottom layer)

1 cup flour

½ cup butter

¼ cup brown sugar

¾ cup chopped pecans

Combine butter and brown sugar while incorporating into flour a bit at a time. Then add pecans. Mixture should then be molded into a 9-inch pie pan. Cook the crust for 15-20 minutes depending on your oven's parameters at 350 degrees (176.6 C). Let cool on counter.

Cream Cheese Layer (second layer)

6 ounces (170 grams) cream cheese, softened

½ cup powdered sugar

2 tablespoons heavy cream (optional: milk or milk substitute)

Mix until smooth and spread over cooled pie crust.

Pudding Layer (third layer)

Vanilla Pudding

<PPP1/3 cup sugar

2 tablespoons cornstarch

1/8 teaspoon salt

2 cups milk

2 large egg yolks, slightly beaten

2 tablespoons butter, softened

2 teaspoons vanilla (or desired flavoring if substituting

Put egg yolks into a heat-resistant bowl. Slightly beat them, then set aside.

In a heavy-duty medium saucepan, combine the sugar, cornstarch, and salt. Mix with a fork or whisk as you gradually stir in milk.

Cook over medium heat, stirring constantly, until mixture thickens and boils. Boil and stir one minute or until thickens. Make sure you continue to stir so that it doesn't burn.

Remove from heat and slowly stir at least half

of the hot mixture into egg yolks. Place the pot back onto the stove, and then stir the hot egg mixture into the saucepan with the remaining mix. Return to a boil while stirring for approximately one minute until all incorporated.

Remove pan from heat.

Stir in the softened butter and vanilla.

Transfer to a bowl and allow to cool or if you are still making the pie crusts, cover and set in the fridge. This step is mainly so you won't eat it!

Whipped Cream (fourth/top layer)

After the pudding is set and cold, top with whipped cream.

If you want the pie to be chocolate, use these instructions for the pudding layer.

Chocolate Pudding

1/2 cup sugar

1/3 cocoa

2 tablespoons cornstarch

1/8 teaspoon salt

2 cups milk

2 large egg yolks, slightly beaten

2 teaspoons vanilla

Put egg yolks into a heat-resistant bowl. Slightly beat them, then set aside.

In a heavy-duty medium saucepan, combine the sugar, cornstarch, and salt. Mix together with a fork or whisk as you gradually stir in milk.

Cook over medium heat, stirring constantly, until mixture thickens and boils. Boil and stir one minute or until thickens. Make sure you continue to stir so that it doesn't burn.

Remove from heat and slowly stir at least half of the hot mixture into egg yolks. Place the pot back onto the stove, and then stir the hot egg mixture into the saucepan with the remaining mix. Return to a boil while stirring for approximately one minute until all incorporated.

Remove the pan from heat.

Stir in the vanilla.

A bit of trivia about the wonderful nut known as the pecan

There's always a lot of back and forth on how to

pronounce this nut from Texas. I have to say that I, and many other Texans, have always pronounced it "pa (pah sounding) con." Whereas you'll find people from up north or in other states pronouncing it "pe (pee) can".

Um, what?

Even search engines show it as puh-kaan or pih-kahn.

So now you know.

www.ingramcontent.com/pod-product-compliance
Lightning Source LLC
Chambersburg PA
CBHW050838190726
48286CB00007B/2138